TEEN INC.

To my father,
who spent most of his life
railing against the machine.
I guess some of it rubbed off . . .

I

THERE'S NO "I" IN TEEN

Ever wonder what'd happen if everyone just stopped believing in money? After all, it's only worth something because people think it is. It's not food, which people need, or gold, which people like. It's just paper. Heck, for the most part it isn't even paper, it's just a record on some computer bank. Can't get more nothing than that. The whole world's economy runs on a shared illusion. It's totally Zen. Go figure.

So, what if everyone one day said, "Hey! This is paper! I'm doing all this work for paper! What am I, out of my freaking head?"

And—*poof*—no more money.

Would it be a cooler world? I dunno. Would it be worse? Doubt it. But it sure would be different. Especially for all those corporations out there running things. Corporations, after all, are big machines designed to make money. In fact, they're legally *obligated* to try to make money. Like, if

Exxon or PepsiCo had a choice between saving some guy who was drowning or making money, they'd be obligated to let the guy drown.

Weird, huh?

This is the kind of thing I think to myself sometimes, especially when I'm headed to a morning meeting. Waking up early on a school day puts me in a bad mood to begin with, and who needs the extra stress? I mean, I just turned fourteen, I'm not six. I'm not even ten. I can't believe I even have to show up for these things anymore.

But I do, so I went, trudging out of my office suite, past the gang in Marketing & PR, and right on down the hall to pain-in-the-ass central.

I knew there was going to be trouble the minute I opened the thick glass door to the conference room. The place was packed. Every seat had a manager in it. My meetings were never this well attended. They were all sipping from Styrofoam coffee cups or plastic water bottles. Despite all the people, it was so quiet you could hear every freaking slurp. If you closed your eyes, it sounded like you were in a swamp.

They also had one of those really cool, giant touch-screen setups. You know, the kind you connect to your laptop? Instead of clicking, you touch it, and there's a special pen you can actually write on it with? They only use that when they really want my attention. So, like I said, trouble.

At first I figured it was going to be yet another homework presentation or a lecture on how I should stay in my room after hours and not wander the halls because it freaks security, complete with a video of me playing hand-ball in the parking lot, but it wasn't.

It was worse.

I made my way to the seat at the head of the table, sleepily waving to Nancy Alein. She'd been my manager, or rather, the head of the department that managed me, for about ten months. Nice enough person, but stiff, stiff, stiff. Always wore suits, even on casual day, blouse buttoned up to the neck. You know the type? Didn't like "messes."

I, of course, much in the same way corporations exist for money, am pretty much by obligation a mess.

Nancy gave me a curt nod. As soon as I sat in my nice cushy chair, she turned on the big screen. No intros, no nothing. That's Nancy, all business.

Page one of a PowerPoint presentation lit the room, with foot-high letters:

Jaiden Beale Dating Options 1Q

My eyes nearly popped out of my head, raced down the hall, and jumped out the window to their grisly death.

"No!" I shouted. "No way! We are *not* going to talk about who I date!"

Nancy held up her hand like a traffic cop. "Jaiden, please. Bob, weren't we supposed to cut that front page? Why wasn't it cut?"

"Sorry. There was a rush . . ."

Furious, I headed for the door, determined to force my

3

whole body through the glass. Nancy, legal pad in hand, leaped to her feet and raced me.

"Jaiden, we're not going to tell you anything," she said. "We'll just facilitate . . ."

"Offer support . . . ," said Bob, cutting in. He's one of the other managers.

Cutting off Nancy is a bad idea. It's a thing with her. She gave old Bob a laser glare that melted him in his seat. He's not an idea man anyway. I'm not sure what he does, other than rephrase whatever the person talking before him says. Staring at him, she finished her sentence, ". . . the process for you."

They had ways of making my life tough if I didn't cooperate, lots of ways—no DVDs, video games, Internet time, no "screens" as Nancy liked to sum it up.

I trudged back to my seat. I looked at my shoes. I looked at the wall. I looked back at the screen. I banged my head against the table. After the last whack, I kept my forehead down and looked up. Through my hair, I saw everyone waiting.

Nancy stepped up to the screen and pressed her finger against a spot. A picture of a kind of familiar blond girl with curly hair appeared. On the right was a list of stats, like her name (Donna something), her year, her interests, her grades. It was kind of like a MySpace page, only with more detail. I twisted my head to the side for a better look.

Nancy cleared her throat and went into her prepared

remarks. I hate those. I wish they'd just send me a memo so I could decide not to read it. She said, "We're here because your last HR evaluation indicated that although you're doing okay academically, socially you're, to put it bluntly, a little less advanced than your peers. Realizing this particular aspect of your transition to public school can be tough, we thought we'd pitch in and take a look at some potential . . . friends."

I pointed at the screen. "Guys, that's a diary entry up there, and her personal chat-room handles. Isn't this like an invasion of privacy?" I said.

"It's like it, but it's not," Nancy explained. That was about it for her sense of humor. Hope you enjoyed it as much as I did. "All this data is public. Your demographic . . . um . . . people your age tend to put a lot of personal info on the Web, thinking it's somehow private. Some of your fellow students probably do this for themselves. We just did a little typing to assemble it for you."

"Because I'm too stupid or lame to make friends myself?"

"No," she said. She extended the *o* to make it sound like a three-syllable word. "We're all very, very proud of you, and genuinely pleased with the strides you've made."

Everyone, I mean everyone, nodded supportively, like they were a bunch of bobble heads on one big corporate body, which is funny if you think about it because the root of corporate means to give something a body, and if anything, a corporation really has no physical body, making it kind of *in*corporeal. Anyway, when they do that I feel like I'm talking to an alien group-mind like in *Invasion of the Body Snatchers*.

"Adolescence is an awkward time," this other guy, Jack Minger, offered. Jack's not so bad. Has kids of his own. Thinks he knows just how to lie to us. "We all go through it, well, most of us."

The "most of us" crack got a few chuckles but Nancy chimed in before any big laugh riots could ensue. "Just look. No pressure. Just . . . fun." she said. Her shoulders shivered. They shivered whenever she said *fun*, as if she were saying *vomit*.

She turned back to the screen. "Donna Maybridge. Same age, same grade. Also just started at Deever High this year. Likes science fiction and *South Park*. You have lunch the same period so there's a perfect chance to interface."

She looked back at me and waited, as if I were going to say something like, "she's the girl for me" but I just raised my eyebrows and let her think it meant whatever.

She pressed the screen again. A sour-faced girl with curly black hair appeared.

"Shanna Denton?" I blurted out. "No way! That girl wants to kill me!"

Well, she did. Ever since that day she came to class wearing a Hello Kitty T-shirt and I said, "Hey, nice shirt."

That's all I said, I swear. I wasn't trying to be sarcastic, just friendly, really, and it's like now I have this death stalker for life.

Nancy wisely touched the screen again.

Secretly, I hoped one of their choices might be Jenny Tate. It'd be sweet to be "forced" to talk to her. I could just tell them she was cool, and they'd fall all over themselves to get me a file. But no way would I say anything about her to the suits. It's hard enough to keep from acting like a lame washout, wimpy sad-ass zombie loser whenever she's in eye range. Knowing more about her would only make me more nervous.

But Jenny wasn't next. Instead, the screen filled with the image of a dark-skinned girl with long black hair. "Caitlin Fermelli. She's a little more academically inclined than you are, taking three honors classes, but you do have similar tastes in music. We were hoping her study habits might rub off on you."

I knew her, but I wasn't interested. Even so, I mentally made a note of her chat-room handle: beeswax29.

So it went, one profile after another, like I was a sultan reviewing women who'd applied for my harem, or a director auditioning starlets. By the end of the meeting I still felt totally stupid, but I like to think my sense of stupidity filled the room and infected everyone.

At long, long last, Nancy glanced at her watch. "Time. Jaiden, I have printouts prepared. Before you run off, this is important. Should you decide to follow up, there's some information we'll have to review about dating etiquette, substance abuse, abstinence as a healthy choice, and, if necessary, the proper use of a condom . . ."

"Jeez!" I screamed. I put my hand over my ears and tore into the hall, dying to put some mileage between myself and Team Awkward.

Unless you haven't been paying attention, you've probably figured out by now that my name's Jaiden. This is not because I had a grandfather named Jaiden, or because I looked like a Jaiden. I got the name because of a naming committee that met three times fourteen years ago. After a lot of back-and-forth, they outsourced the project to a branding firm. The branding firm came up with Jaiden.

If you're a time traveler from the dawn of the Industrial Revolution and think a company is something that makes *things*, a branding firm is a little hard to understand. Their "product" as they like to call it, is ideas. They sit around all day coming up with names and designs ("customer experiences") they think people will remember—like for Prozac, the antidepressant drug. That name was invented by a company called Interbrand. It was a combination of *pro*, meaning "positive," and *zac*, suggesting exactness, or precision. Take it and you become "exactly positive." Get it? If you think that's strange, remind me to tell you what a corporate-identity specialist does. No lie, it's a real job.

Anyway, Interbrand was too expensive, so I'm the only

human being in the whole world named by LogoStrong, the company that came up with Um-drops, the gentle yet effective laxative. So, Jaiden it was. Jaiden Beale. Beale, they couldn't decide on, in committee or otherwise. It was my parents' last name. Other than my genes, "Beale" was all my parents left me.

Oh, yeah. That and a forty-million-dollar wrongful death settlement.

But I can't touch a penny until I'm twenty-five. Until then, NECorp, the company responsible for killing them, is my legal guardian, my parent corporation if you will.

Wacky world, huh?

To be fair, it wasn't NECorp, exactly, it was SafeWarm, a fully owned and operated subsidiary, that produced the faulty gas valve that caused the kitchen explosion that killed Mom and Dad. To be even more specific, there was this floor manager, Dan Blake, a real mover and shaker. Not a very patient guy either. He made some changes to the production process that could've safely doubled the valve production, but he was out to make a name for himself, so he quadrupled it, speeding things up to a point where a bad valve slipped through Quality Assurance.

They fired his ass. I don't know what happened to him after that, but I like to think he goes from job to job, getting his ass fired, like a damned spirit, condemned to wander the earth searching for his lost, I dunno, his lost ass, I guess.

The explosion happened two days after my parents brought me home, unnamed, from the hospital. According to the news accounts, they were heating a bottle for me at the time. The blast took out half the house. Me and the nursery were in the other half.

It was a huge, huge scandal. I didn't have any other family, but the high-powered law firm of Helson, Holtz and Mannifeld saw an opportunity to win fame and fortune, so they represented me while I was put up for adoption.

Many heads rolled aside from Dan's. Stock dropped. SafeWarm was sort of put to death. Actually, it was disbanded, its pieces sold. If you ask me, old Dan should have been disbanded and had *his* pieces sold, instead of just being fired.

The press was all over it for weeks and NECorp was afraid the court case would destroy them, until their CEO, Mr. Desmond Hammond III, came up with this truly whacked idea. He offered a big payout on the condition that NECorp be allowed to raise me. He pointed out that I didn't have parents anyway, and wouldn't it be hard to be certain that whoever wanted to adopt me wasn't just in it for the money and fame?

It was a kind of a PR, sleight-of-hand thing. Instead of thinking about poor parentless me and how I should have forty billion instead of forty million, questions started flying about whether a corporation could raise a child.

It was brilliant. Mr. Hammond is a crazed genius type,

famous for engineering NECorp's explosive growth, but also famous for being totally weird and, lately, for having a tendency to agree with whomever he spoke to last, whether it was a janitor, or the blue jay that landed on his window ledge.

NECorp promised to give me the best upbringing possible. When they outlined the specifics—the well-rounded education I'd get, the care and affection—my attorneys started listening, and, after securing their own big payback, said yes.

For the nitpickers among us, technically, I don't think I was adopted directly by NECorp. A corporation is a legal person under the law, with the same rights and (supposedly) responsibilities, so you'd think maybe having one adopt a kid wouldn't be quite so weird. But it turns out that lots of states have adoption laws that define people as the flesh-and-blood kind.

There are, however, a few states that have no such legal definition, and it was in one of those states that NECorp created The Jaiden Beale Fellowship, Inc., another fully owned and operated subsidy, and I think, technically, it's that entity that is my "biological" parent corporation. That's the closest I understand it, anyway. Some guy from Legal once explained it, but, really, it made my head spin.

I'm sure having one or two parents try to figure out how to raise you sucks sometimes, but trust me, steering committees, focus groups, and upper-level executives approving everything is way worse. Just one example? It took three months and twenty memos before I was allowed to watch my first episode of *South Park*—and it wasn't even that funny. At that rate, I'd be seventeen before I get permission to see an R-rated movie, and by then I wouldn't need permission.

So sometimes I wish that people would stop believing in money and that NECorp would just go away.

By the time I made it to the cafeteria, I had ten minutes before I had to catch my bus, so I raced up to Ben at the grill. Sometimes, I get a few stares from visitors, but they're quickly told who I am. I feel more comfortable on Fridays, casual day, since my T-shirt and jeans don't stand out quite so much.

"The usual?" Ben said. He's my man. Kind of short, about my height of five feet five inches, so we see eye to eye. He's stocky as all hell, though, so you wouldn't want to cross him. Been making me breakfast weekdays for five years. He's got this mellow way of doing everything, cracking eggs, swishing the whisk, flipping the home fries. I love to watch him cook. He's like a Zen master of cholesterol.

I nodded and he tossed some fresh bacon on the grill. That great sizzling, salty smell woke me up a bit, and I finally started to forget about the meeting.

That is, until Ben smiled and asked, "How'd the dating game go?"

If it was anyone else talking, I'd have walked. "You get a memo?"

He shook his head and gave me a mysterious smile. "I don't need a memo. I keep telling you everyone likes to talk while they're waiting on line. If you were listening, you'd have known about it days ago. How bad was it?"

"Picture the worst, double it, then bury it until it stinks."

He slid a clean plate out and gave me a look. "Want them to stop?"

"Hell, yeah."

"Ask a girl out yourself."

"Right."

"Be smart," Ben said. "Their job is to make sure you reach certain benchmarks. It's like quotas, sales figures for them. You make the goals, they leave you alone, but the longer it takes, the more their jobs are at risk, so the more they have to get involved. Remember what happened when you were failing math last year?"

How could I forget? Nancy, in one of her least endearing moves, decided I should be sent on a retreat with accounting. You haven't lived until you've had forced bonding with twenty high-level accountants.

"Hold that thought," Ben said as he flipped my eggs. "Now ask yourself if it would be so awful to ask some girl, even just a friend you like, to go to a movie?"

I gave him a shrug. "I'll take it under advisement."

He always talked sense. That's why I liked him so

much. That's also probably why he's a short-order cook. The more sense you make around here, the less they pay you.

To get the really high-paying jobs, you have to be totally nuts.

2

MEANWHILE, OUTSIDE THE BOX

I scarfed down my breakfast, even the home fries, which I hate to do, because I love them more than life itself. Then I booked across the lobby, said a quick hello to the guard, opened the doors, and entered what is still sometimes referred to as the real world.

The nine-to-fivers were just arriving, streaming in from the expressway, making the parking lot a mess. When I'm on time, I avoid the crunch. Now I had to dodge tons of cars. My goal was a housing development beyond a small patch of trees on the far end of NECorp. That's where the school bus picked me up, so no one would see where I lived.

NECorp's world corporate headquarters is a humongous white building surrounded by an artificial lake. Its got towers, sleek flat surfaces, two domes, huge windows the size of countries, and abstract fountains and statues all over the place. Looks like a cool retro spaceship from the otherwise boring old movie, *2001: A Space Odyssey*.

The moon is cool, too, but you don't want anyone thinking you live there, right? Which brings me to the fact that in school, my "true" identity was a secret, shared with no one. Yeah, I know, I'm no Spider-Man, and there were all those news stories about me, so you'd think anonymity would be impossible, but my adoption was over a decade ago, and the press basically got tired of me after I learned to walk. Sure, anyone could figure out who I was if they wanted to, but so far no one wanted to. I was, in the meantime, free to hide in plain sight.

Just as the bus showed up, I stumbled out from the trees and scrambled up the steps, the doors *phishing* shut behind me. Nate Buckman, ultimate computer freak, was on board as usual.

"Beale!" he called out in a deep voice. He put his fancy handheld PDA in his lap and high-fived me as I sat next to him. His voice was the only thing about him that was deep. He was a short, thin, bookish kid with glasses. He also had these kind of fat, chunky cheeks and buckteeth. In grade school they called him "Chipmunk Cheeks."

Since I was his friend, I just called him Nate.

Honestly, I thought of him as totally normal, compared to me. In fact, Nate was my image of what a normal kid should be. Except maybe for the teeth. We started talking on the bus the first day of school and found out we liked the same kind of music, the same science fiction, the same video games, and not the same girls, so we got along great.

Speaking of which . . .

"Still like Caitlin?" I asked him.

"As long as I'm still breathing," he said as he absently surfed the Web.

I nudged him. "Well, what if you knew her screen name at TeenTime.com?"

He made a face. "What if monkeys flew out of my butt and handed me a winning lottery ticket?"

I took out a pen and scribbled *beeswax29* on his notebook.

His eyes lit up, and he actually put the PDA down. "No way!"

"Yes," I said, with utmost somberness. "It is indeed, way."

He looked at the scribble again, then back at me. "For real? I owe you, like, my liver! Wait? What am I going to say to her? What can I talk about? I can't believe this!"

He went on like that for the rest of the ride. His voice even jumped an octave once or twice. It almost made the whole ugly meeting worthwhile, except for the excruciating embarrassment. Eventually we arrived at the school.

As a building, Deever High is not so great. It's old, I know because the cornerstone I pass on the way in every day says 1953, which I think puts its birth in the middle of the Red Scare or the Korean War, or both, a time when I guess everyone was too busy fighting something to care much about how best to build high schools. It's got this weird brick-and-steel construction that looks like it came out of a toy box, and everything inside smells gross, a combination of sneakers, paint, sour milk, mold; you know the drill. The entrance doors have like a million coats of aqua paint on them that's so ugly you'd think they'd have stopped making it long before you could put a million coats of it on anything.

But I loved it more than anyplace I'd ever seen, because, even with the work, the occasional lousy teacher, and the bullies, it was the only place in my whole corporate existence where I felt almost normal.

I said good-bye to Nate, who was so busy making notes on his PDA on what to say to Caitlin that he didn't even notice, and headed for homeroom. The rest of the morning was pretty dull, except maybe for a moment during second period art history where Shanna Denton, as usual, kept giving me the evil eye. Sometimes I'm afraid she's actually going to kill me because of that Hello Kitty thing. Her skin just oozed hatred for me. It made me feel like actually reading the file Nancy had given me on her, just to get some juicy gossip, but I figured ultimately it would only get me into more trouble.

Third period bio was when my blood pressure always shot up. Not because I really loved biology, or the teacher, Ms. Chrob, who was as affable as a sack of potatoes and looked like one, too. I barely paid attention to her, but bio was the class I shared with Jenny Tate. She always sat by the windows way in the front, I always sat against the wall way in the back. I liked to think of it as "our" class. *Ha*.

But what could I say about Jenny, really, since I'd never even spoken to her? I wished I knew something about her other than her name and the way she looked, but I bet whatever else there was to know was really great, too. I planned to actually say hello to her someday, to break the ice or whatever. Much as Nate was my buddy, my giving him Caitlin's screen handle was also a little experiment. I wanted to see how Nate would handle it and what would happen. If it worked out for him, hey, why not me?

When Jenny wasn't already in her seat when I arrived, I was briefly bummed, thinking she might be absent. But then I got this tingle at the back of my head, a sort of Jenny-radar, and in she walked. She was wearing a short orangey blouse that I guess would usually expose her midriff, but she had a sweater tied around her waist, so no skin in sight.

I was vaguely aware that Ms. Chrob had started talking: "Looks like everyone's here, so before we begin our review of the digestive system . . ."

Or something like that. Anyway, Jenny had this light skin with tons of freckles, really clean red hair, and bright green eyes. I mean green you could spot from halfway down the hall.

"I want to give you your assignments for our project this year, but first, a warning. One year we had two students bring in the heart of a dog for a project on the circulatory system. We're still not sure where they got it, but since then the school has had a strict models-only policy."

When Jenny shifted, moving further into the light of the sun, the skin on her face totally vanished, but you could still make out her freckles, like little backward stars, dark against light.

"You'll be paired up into randomly assigned teams, to give everyone an opportunity to actually do the work instead of socializing."

Suddenly, Jenny's head turned and I caught a flash of those green eyes. It was like she felt me thinking about her the same way I could sense it when she walked into the room. Or maybe the sun was getting to be too much. Either way, I couldn't bear it, so I turned away quickly.

Those rare moments when Jenny was facing me were the only times I ever looked at Ms. Chrob. Don't get me wrong. Despite appearances I am not a bad student. It was usually pretty easy to catch up with whatever Chrob was talking about. She repeated it often enough, like we were idiots. Like right then I knew she was talking about that stupid project she'd only mentioned a billion times. Now, she was reading out the names of the teams.

"Drevin and Gallancy," she said. "Bergstom and Perry."

Of course you know what I was wishing for and dreading. Wishing for, because I really wanted it; dreading it because I knew if it happened, I'd wind up acting like a total idiot and ruining everything forever. At least when something's a fantasy, it's still possible, you know? You can pretend forever that you have something to look forward to.

Likewise, I never thought in a million years the universe would ever organize itself around my daydreams. Mostly it seemed like things happened regardless of what I wanted, like that great meeting this morning. But every now and then . . .

"Tate and Beale."

For a few seconds, I thought I was wishing it so hard that I'd hallucinated. I briefly feared that I was crazy now, forever stuck inside a dream.

But it did happen. I had heard it.

Jenny Tate was going to be my project partner! For a month!

I hoped to hell I wasn't grinning like an idiot. I was still staring at the front of the classroom, but I realized I had to do something to avoid seeming like a loser right off the bat. I had to look at her and smile or nod or wink. No, not winking. That would be ridiculous. Just look and nod. Look and nod.

Only I couldn't. You ever stop to think about how many thoughts and muscles it takes to do a precision movement like turn your head, make eye contact with someone, and nod? If you really think about it, you'll wonder how it ever happens.

All of a sudden, I wished I'd had Nancy there with me

giving me a PowerPoint presentation on how to move my neck.

First, twist your head as shown here. If you don't get it the first time, click on the illustration to see the process again.

Seconds ticked by. Soon it would be too late, or late enough for whatever I did to look really weird, like I was stuck in a time delay like when they interview someone half a world away and you have this ungodly pause between the question and the answer.

Summoning all my will, I swallowed and turned, just like in the PowerPoint illustration I imagined. Jenny was already looking at me, like maybe she hadn't even stopped from before they announced our names. I think I smiled, but I definitely nodded. She smiled and nodded back.

There's this movie called *Contact* with Jodie Foster, where she meets an alien species for the first time, and there's this huge gulf between them and it's really tough for them to figure out how to communicate.

It was sort of like that.

The rest of class I was afraid to even look at her. So I looked at Chrob. I even listened to her. I took notes. I understood things about cellular structure—the nucleus, the cell wall, protoplasm, the endoplasmic reticulum, which is kind of a circulatory system inside the individual cell. I was feeling focused, academic, like maybe I wanted to study biology in college.

Then the bell rang.

Everyone shifted out of their seats. I stood up very carefully in case Jenny was still watching. After all, I didn't want her to see me fall down or anything.

There she was, walking up to me.

"So . . . ," I said. She smiled again, and waited for me to finish whatever it was I was going to say. Unfortunately, I had no idea what that was.

Another word. Say another word. Make a sentence.

"We're going to be working together, huh?"

"Looks that way," she said. "Any idea which project you want to do?"

No. Say no.

"Uh . . . nope."

"Me neither. Maybe we should get together like this weekend and get started?"

Together? Of course, together! It's a group project, idiot! Okay, talk again now.

"You mean like Saturday?"

She looked worried. "Is that too soon? That's not cool, is it? I'm not very cool. I get that from my family. And now I'm talking too much."

What do I say? I can't tell her I think she's cool, that wouldn't be cool . . .

"Yes. No. I mean this weekend is fine. Totally fine. And cool."

She laughed a little. "Don't you live near Westerly Avenue? My cousin Madge lives around there, and she's seen you get on the bus. I could bike over and meet you at your house."

"Sure. Great. What time?" I managed.

I forgot what time she mentioned, but it didn't matter. I could ask later, after I had more practice actually speaking to her. Right then, all I had to do was get away without tripping or drooling or bursting into hysterical laughter. I smiled again, not too weirdly, I hoped, exited the class, and turned a hallway corner. Checking to make sure she hadn't followed, I jumped into the air, then pounded my feet into the floor one after the other until it felt like my toes would fall off.

Jenny Tate was going to be my project partner, and she wanted to work at my house!

It wasn't turning out to be such a bad day at all.

In fact, it was probably the best day I'd ever had.

Now the only problem was, where was I going to get a house?

3

HOME SUITE HOME

My "room" is a converted office suite in Area 2B, which can be found toward the back of the PR department. It's near a service elevator, so sometimes you'll get banging when something's loaded or unloaded, but otherwise it's pretty private. It used to belong to Dave Laconte, a Super-Creep Veep who suddenly "retired." Never heard the whole story. Probably one of those boring embezzlement things. Just once I'd like to see someone fired because he's secretly a lycanthrope that's slaughtering townsfolk.

In my room, there's a big white open area with lots of windows where I keep my bed, a cool plasma TV hooked up with a PS3, and some other junk. Then there's a smaller room with my desk, for studying and reading. I guess if it wasn't mine, and didn't look so much like what it was, an office suite, I'd think it was pretty great.

I was thinking, for a whole wild and crazy afternoon, that I'd just come out and tell Jenny my life story, reveal my identity, so to speak. If I were a superhero, that'd be exactly the sort of thing that'd impress a girl. "You see, Jenny, I secretly fight crime with the radioactive strength of a megaconglomerate."

But, no.

After school, I went straight to good old Area 2B and took a long hard look at it. Over the years, I'd managed to cover a lot of the paneling (called "Executive Burl") with posters and whatnot, but no matter what, especially with that romantic view of the parking lot, it still looked like a freaking office. I tried rearranging, sort of making my bed, kicking the clothes into one or two piles instead of six or seven. But it was hopeless.

I couldn't bring Jenny to NECorp. She'd freak and run.

I keep a bunch of model spaceships on some shelves. I hadn't played with them in years. I picked one up to look at. What I thought was some nice detail painting of an oil smudge turned out to be dust, which only served to remind me how long I'd been here. That got me to feeling sorry for myself, which got me to thinking about sucky life in general as it applied to my sucky life in specific.

When I was a kid and I actually played with those models, I used to pretend I had my own TV show. It was a talk show, a weekly vehicle for my spontaneous wit and engaging patter. Sometimes, I'd interview my favorite people, like Mahatma Gandhi or the Incredible Hulk, who I think are both really interesting, but in different ways.

I said I was a kid, okay?

I canceled the show about two years ago because I was looking for other projects, and, well, it started feeling stupid pretending I was on TV. But I do still like to imagine that someday someone will ask what it was like to be the first kid raised by a corporation.

It could happen. It's a lot more likely than the werewolf thing.

So, I figured I should have some sort of prepared answer. For the longest time, the stuff I came up with was your standard garbage, like, "Well, Bob, or Barbara, it was a unique and edifying experience with many challenges that made me a stronger person." That sort of crap. Then, in my first few weeks at Deever, I came up with a real answer.

It happened thanks to Mr. Banyon's English class. We were reading classic science fiction. At first I thought this would be cool, but it turned out to be mostly about "idea-driven" books, stories by people with names like Asimov and Ellison. I got into them, but they lacked the sort of cosmic-scale explosions that generally keep my attention.

We also had to read two "seminal" novels, *1984*, by George Orwell, and *Brave New World*, by Aldous Huxley. Neither had any explosions, just all this dystopian stuff about where society was headed in the grim future and how gross we are as a species.

For our paper, my first big paper, we had to compare

them. Jack Minger, who was managing my homework at the time, offered to prep me, but I felt like I should do all the work myself. (See? I told you I wasn't a bad student.) I thought long and hard, and the thing I came up with was that both of the main characters died, but in opposite ways.

In *1984*, the government runs everything like a really bad corporation. They make it, they own it, they distribute it, and you do what they tell you. The government's cruel about it, too, outlawing any personal freedom. Like the book says, if it's not compulsory, it's forbidden. It also watches everyone all the time and tries to control their every move. They even had a logo, Big Brother, the guy supposed to be doing the watching, sort of the ultimate in dark branding. The main character, Winston Smith, tries to rebel, but they catch him and torture him. Eventually he just gives up and says okay, everything's really great with the way you guys run things. I love Big Brother, I really do. So they stop torturing him and shoot him in the back of the head. The end.

Cheery, huh?

Brave New World was the opposite. Instead of gray and poor and deeply sad, everything was bright and shiny and totally shallow. People were born out of tubes and never knew their parents, so sex was just for fun. The government wasn't cruel, but all the people were clueless (like Mr. Hammond, the CEO). Anyway, they found this guy, John, living in some part of the world they thought was unpopulated. He was raised the way people used to be, with a birth mother, which they thought was horribly gross, and given the birth video I saw once in hygiene, I tend to agree with them.

John tries to get used to all this entertainment and drugs and sex, but he can't, so he kills himself, and everyone says, "Oh, what a shame he couldn't adapt to our totally cool world" and they go back to their video games. (By the way, I think M. T. Anderson's *Feed* was better than both these books, but it wasn't a choice in the assignment.) My big comparison was about how Winston Smith was killed and Savage John killed himself, but they both wound up dead. I got an A.

Long story short, I guess what I'll say to my interviewer is that being raised by a corporation is like a cross between *Brave New World* and *1984*. There's this big powerful thing with vast resources watching you all the time, but rather than torture you, it's trying to figure out what you like, only it's really too shallow and goofy to ever do that.

Thinking about all that megagoofiness got me thinking about those vast resources. NECorp had holdings in like a gazillion companies. It owned at least one of everything. So, a crazy idea jammed up my frontal lobe.

I raced out of my room, ran down the corridor, and hit the elevator button. I almost never hit it more than once. I hate it when people do that, even if they're in a hurry. It's like throwing rocks at your dog because he's not running happily toward you fast enough.

Anyway, when the elevator didn't come fast enough, I hit the steps and ran all the way to Nancy's office and walked right in, since I'm allowed.

Nancy was at her desk, typing like crazy. It was all about the work with her. In fact, there wasn't a single picture or photo in the room, just her.

She kept at it as I stood there, but did raise the index finger of her right hand. Her other fingers, even those on the same hand, kept typing, and she didn't turn her head. This was Nancy-speak for, *I know you're there and will interface with you shortly.*

Finally, she said, "Jaiden" and clicked a few more keys. "You're supposed to be in the gym. We discussed how you can't cut back on your workouts until after you're on one of the school teams. Now . . ."

I waved my hands frantically in front of me, which is Jaiden-speak for *Not now please, I have another subject I wish to discuss.*

She looked at me. She loved the schedule like it was her best friend in the world, but at the same time she was smart enough to know working with me required flexibility. You could see her brain rifle through the possible things I could get excited about. When she picked the one she liked best, she said, "Did you pick someone from the files?"

"Uh, no. Not exactly. Do we own any houses?"

She raised an eyebrow. "We own factories, mansions,

airplanes, helicopters, huge tracts of land in third world countries . . ."

I waved my hands again briefly.

"I mean, does NECorp own any normal houses that normal people might live in somewhere in this school district, preferably in this neighborhood?"

That got her curiosity up, one of her few emotions. "What's this about?"

I stonewalled, which means I didn't answer her question. "Do we?"

"There's a house over on Westerly for visiting execs and transfers."

I was so excited, I started shaking like a little kid. "Can I have it?"

"Define 'have it.'"

"Okay, look, there's a girl, Jenny Tate, who's my partner for a bio project, and she wants to come over to see my house."

"Ah," she said.

"Ah" is Nancy-speak for *I understand exactly where this conversation is going, but why don't you say it out loud anyway to prove I'm right?*

"And I really don't want her to see *this* house," I concluded.

It was a long hard fight to get NECorp to allow me to go to public school, something I'd wanted since I was eight. Early on, I had tutors. When my social development proved to be lagging, I was sent to very expensive but totally sterile private schools, where, more and more, I sucked at everything.

When I turned thirteen, a Psych Committee report indicated I had early symptoms of depression (like half the world). That was when they 'caved on the public school thing. If I wound up clinically depressed, NECorp could be held accountable by both the courts and the press. So, once I was ready for ninth grade, my biggest wish was granted, and I started attending Deever, making me, at least during school days, almost a real person.

Nancy, knowing all this, asked, "Is Jenny from one of the files?"

"No."

She seemed disappointed, which I understood since compiling those files was hard work.

"So, is she someone you . . . want to get to know better?"

I rolled my eyes and shifted on my feet.

She *tsk*ed in annoyance. "Is she someone you like or want to be friends with? How do you want me to say it?"

I folded my arms over my chest. "I think the bottom line is I really don't want you to say it at all, but now that you have we both know what you mean, so you can stop."

"Fine. Look, Jaiden, it's perfectly natural that at this time of your life . . ."

"Yes! Got it! I know the trends. I know where I fit on

the bell curve. I even know the lyrics to 'Teenage Waste-land.' I just don't want to feel like I'm in a nature show, okay?"

"Okay. How soon would you need the house?"

I gave her a double take. "You'll get it for me?"

"I can check and see if it's empty."

"Really? What's it like?"

She tapped a few keys and whirled her screen toward me. "Like this. A furnished three-bedroom colonial."

"Perfect! What about parents?"

Nancy did a double take. "Excuse me? Parents?"

"It'd be pretty strange if I was living there alone, right?"

Nancy sighed and clicked a few more keys. "I was going to work Saturday anyway. I can bring my quarterlies and be there for maybe three hours. If I sat there and worked and said, hi, without actually claiming to be related to you, I don't think we'd be open to any liability. I'll have to run it by Legal . . ."

The bit about Legal should have told me right off there'd be trouble, but I was way too excited to really think it through. "Great! Thank you!"

She pointed at me again with that index finger. "I'm not going to make you and your friend any snacks. I don't do snacks. The results would be pleasing for neither of us. I'll grunt pleasantly when you introduce us and then we leave each other alone. Agreed?"

"Perfect, that'd be totally perfect. What about a dad?"

She scrunched her face. "Don't push it. It's a single-parent household."

"Really? I just think it would be more normal if I had . . ."

She cut me off with her hand. Then, all of a sudden, out of absolutely nowhere, she got this expression I'd never seen on her before. She looked . . . sympathetic.

"Jaiden, you don't have parents. What you have is a multinational conglomerate charged with overseeing your development, and your adoption is a matter of public record. Anyone who wants to can figure it out. It's great you've got a date, really, and I'll try and make that as easy for you as possible, but you really have to start thinking about what you'll do when the news breaks at your school, which will happen sooner or later."

That was a bummer. No *1984*, but close.

I looked down at my sneakers. "I know. I'm just kind of hoping it can be later."

Then we had another first for Nancy. She smiled.

"Then worry about it later. I'll make some calls and get back to you."

4

A FEARFUL SYNERGY

Next morning when I reached the head of the breakfast line, Ben stopped cooking and looked at me funny.

"What?" I said, thinking my hair was messed up.

"There's something different," he said, cracking eggs into a bowl. "Something . . ."

He picked up a whisk and beat the eggs until they were frothy. "Not a haircut . . . and I know I've seen that T-shirt before. Wait. Got it."

He put down the whisk and snapped his fingers. "You're smiling."

I gave him a look. "You're just torturing me, aren't you? You already know about the bio project and the house and everything, don't you?"

He laughed as he poured the eggs out on the grill, where they sizzled and bubbled.

"Yes, yes I do. All the same, nice to see you in a good mood."

"I hope they don't make me read any reports on dating ethics," I said.

"So it *is* a date?"

"No! I mean, they think it is, and you know how they get and . . ."

He handed me my plate, home fries extra crunchy. "Relax. Have a nice time."

On the bus, I saw Nate. Since I walk home from school, I hadn't since yesterday. So, I told him, not about the fake house, but about Jenny. He actually turned off his PDA and spoke to me, in honor of the auspicious occasion.

"Wow! That's manna from heaven! Karma. First I get Caitlin's screen name, now Jenny's your lab partner," he said. "We should seriously buy some lottery tickets."

Maybe he was right. Maybe we were entering a golden age.

"Did you look up beeswax29?" I asked.

"Sort of," he said.

"Sort of?" I could tell he'd chickened out, but I wanted details.

That deep voice of his went down to a whisper. "I am so lame. I went to the chat room and she was there, but I just watched her name for an hour until she logged off."

"An hour? Dude, that's cyber-stalking!"

"I know. I didn't plan it that way. I just froze. Tonight I'm going to ping her," he said. Then his face went all funny. "You don't suppose this ever gets any easier, do you?"

"Sure," I said. "It's got to."

The bus hit a bump, and he was onto other subjects. "Jenny's coming over, but *I've* never been over. Why don't we hang out at your house sometime?"

My face must have turned chalky, because he laughed. "Not this weekend, stupid. I wouldn't ruin it for you. Next week? I want to see that plasma-screen TV."

"Yeah," I said. "Sure."

But I doubt I looked like I meant it.

That was my first indication this whole thing might not wind up so good. As far as Jenny went, I was hoping after Saturday I could make some excuse so we'd wind up at her house or the library for the remainder of the project, but what was I going to say to Nate? Sorry, I don't really have a house? Why don't you come to HQ sometime and we can raid the office supply cabinet? Need any paper clips? I've got lots and they're free!

By the time bio started and Jenny walked into class, I was feeling better about all the filthy lies. You know I couldn't care less about what I wear, let alone what anyone else does, but there was something about her that made me pay attention to the specifics. I think it was her hair and eyes, red and green, she was just so . . . colorful. I wonder if she had any idea what a great distraction she was.

Anyway, she had on this nice auburn sweater-shirt thing, and after the bell rang, I even managed to walk up and talk to her.

"So, Jenny, Saturday, right?"

"Yeah," she said, nodding. "Where do you live?"

"47 Westerly." I tried not to sound proud about having a street address, but I may have come across a little like a kindergartner reciting his phone number for the first time. "White colonial, blue trim. Not a McMansion, but it's McHome."

"Great. That's only two blocks from my cousin's," she said. Then she made a face. "More not-coolness from me. My dad wants me to make sure your parents will be there."

"No, that's totally cool. My . . . mom will be. Good enough? She'll be working . . . ," I said. It felt weird. It was the first time I'd actually, directly, completely lied to her. I mean, technically the house did belong to my parent-corporation, so it was mine, in a way, but Nancy really wasn't my mother.

"Yeah, that'll be fine. He'll want to call her."

I furrowed my brow, then realized I could give her Nancy's office extension. Why couldn't my mom work for NECorp?

"No problemo."

"What time's good? Noon?"

Ack. Lunchtime. Remembering what Nancy said about snacks, I figured I could get some junk food from the vending machines, but that wouldn't exactly be a meal . . .

"How about after lunch? 1:30?" I said.

"Great," she said.

It was done. I whirled and walked off to math.

Okay, so my chat with Jenny wasn't very deep, but you have to understand I was totally cool the whole time. Did you notice I told a joke? The McMansion thing?

I promised myself I'd talk to her a little more each day, but I wussed out and didn't. That was our longest conversation all week. I did give Jenny Nancy's number, and her dad called. Nancy said it went okay, but there was something about the way she said it that made me think she wasn't telling me everything.

Meanwhile, the rest of the week went like molasses rolling uphill. Nate was expecting me to invite him over and, well, I didn't. He also kept swearing he was going to ping beeswax29, but he never did. I hoped he wasn't getting into stalking her.

I didn't see the house until Saturday morning. Some visiting bigshot was staying there and wasn't out until Friday night. I was nervous about that, but figured it might be better than having the place empty for too long. Houses with people have smells. Not that I wanted it to be full of body odors or weird cooking aromas, I just didn't want it to seem totally unlived in.

After a sleepless Friday night, I got up early and put together a few posters, my laptop, some books, and a spaceship or two for atmosphere. Then I put on a hoodie, got my bike out of the parking lot, and headed over to inspect the place. Westerly was a cul de sac, pretty quiet, so I didn't even pass any cars. Nancy wasn't there yet, so I left my bike on the lawn and used the keys she gave me to open up the front door.

Not too bad—big center hall with a staircase, high ceilings. The furniture was a little hotel-roomish, but passable. There were even paintings on the wall. The biggest problem was that a cleaning crew had already been here, so it looked too clean. I tossed some pillows around, crumpled up some papers and tossed them around, too.

I went upstairs and examined the bedrooms. The master bedroom suite was nice, with a huge whirlpool tub in the bathroom, but I couldn't make that my room. I found a smaller bedroom down the hall that looked about right and stood there at the door, smiling a bit, wondering if Nate had a bedroom like this.

I quickly realized he didn't. No one my age would. The freaking place was spotless and the stuff on the walls was this classical crap with clowns and horses. I yanked those down and put them in the closet, ruffled up the bedspread then set about hanging my posters, plugging in my laptop, and generally trying to make it look like I'd lived in the place for years. I wished there'd been more dust, but what can you do?

I figured if I kept up my imaginary witty banter, Jenny wouldn't notice a thing.

Right.

Nancy showed up at one. I met her at the door.

"Hi, 'Mom'!" I said cheerfully.

She gave me a look, then eyed the papers on the floor. "I told the cleaning service to be done by ten."

"They were here, but I wanted to make the place look more lived in," I explained.

She gave me another look, then moved as if she were going to pick up the papers. About halfway toward the first piece she shook her head. "I'm leaving this all to you. I'll be in the den."

"Okay, great," I said. She sighed and headed off.

"Nancy," I said. She stopped and turned to face me. "Thanks for this, really."

"You're welcome. I hope it goes well. Sure you don't want a file on her? Because, you know . . . ," she said, patting her laptop case.

"Absolutely positive."

I went back to my room and waited. There was a TV, so I tried watching, but mostly I looked at the clock, then out the window at the long empty street.

At one twenty-three, two bicycles appeared. Jenny was riding one of them. A taller girl with blond hair tied in pigtails, rode the other. The cousin, I figured. Madge. They circled the cul de sac, like they were doing reconnaissance work for the army.

At last, Madge headed off. Jenny came up to the lawn, put her bike next to mine, and walked toward the door. I gave everything a final glance and raced out of the room.

I was sweating like crazy. Halfway down the stairs I realized this was probably because I still had on my hoodie. I ripped it off, threw it across the room, and yanked open the door.

It might've looked better if I'd waited until she rang the bell.

"Oh, hi!" I said. "I was just going . . . out . . . to get my bike."

Quick recovery, I thought.

"Hi!" she sang back. No harm, no foul. She was holding her books over her chest in this really cute and girlish way.

"Come in," I said. And she did. Like she was in my power or something.

"Madge, my cousin, was surprised you lived here. She thought it was some kind of corporate house," Jenny said as she looked around.

"Ha!" I said.

I held her books as she took off her sweater. It was the same auburn one she wore during the week. When she handed it to me, I noticed it had a kind of sweet smell.

"Is that watermelon?" I asked, trying to sound suave as I hung up her sweater.

"Yeah," she said, pulling out a roll of hard candy. "Want one?"

As I took the roll, I touched her finger for a second. I popped one in my mouth and nearly swallowed it. I hate watermelon candy, but what the hell.

Right on cue, Nancy stepped out from the den and stuck out her hand. "Hello," she said, like a robot. "You must be Jenny."

I couldn't really blame her for not acting, you know, more human, but I did.

"Hello," Jenny said back. They shook hands and Robot-Mom stepped back. I felt like looking for her remote.

"I'll let you two start your project. I'll be working in . . . here, if you need me," Nancy said. Then she turned and marched off to interface with her robot masters.

It was brief but normal enough.

"So, let's go," I said. I trotted up the stairs and felt her follow.

"This is your room?"

"Yeah. It's okay, isn't it?"

"Okay? It's your room. What difference does it make what I think?" she said. "As long as you're not, you know, polluting the world or making crack cocaine in here."

"Ha," I said again.

She made a beeline for the spaceship. "The Falcon! I love *Star Wars*."

So far so good.

"Me too. Especially the new ones. The old ones look . . . old."

"I really liked *Revenge of the Sith*, but it's so sad," she said. She put her books on my bed and sat next to them. I guess if it really had been my bed it would have felt great to have her and her books on it.

"Do you have the assignment?" she asked.

My eyes went wide. I *knew* I'd forgotten something. "Uh . . . no."

She laughed. "That's okay. I've got my copy."

"Great. I'll boot up, so we can take notes," I said. I popped my laptop's on button.

"Nice rig," she said. "I'm jealous. Dad hates Microsoft so he insists on installing Linux, only he's not very good at it so it never works quite right."

Computer chat was a dead end for me, so I said, "You like *South Park*?"

Her eyes lit up. "I love the one where Cartman tells the Christmas story. You see it?"

"Uh, no. I've only seen a couple of episodes . . ."

One, really. Maybe I should have stuck with computers.

"Why don't we pick our project? Have any favorites?" she asked.

I hadn't even read the list. "Not really. It's hard to choose. They're all so . . . so biological."

She laughed. "There's one on mercury poisoning, if you're into the environment."

I walked over, sat next to her on the bed and we both looked at the list for a really long time. To this day I have no idea what was written on that sheet of paper. I just knew that we were so close I could feel warmth coming off her body. When she shifted a little, to get closer, her hair tickled the side of my face.

"Sorry," she said.

"Uh," I answered. I can be a real wit, huh? I looked at her and she smiled.

So we were sitting there, smiling. It was the kind of moment where if this was a movie, the guy would lean forward, then the girl would lean forward, then they'd both pause a second, look at each other, lean forward some more and wind up swapping spit.

But Jenny and I just sat there smiling.

"Jaiden!"

I thought about moving forward, but couldn't.

"Jaiden!"

"Um, Jaiden, I think your mom's calling you," Jenny said.

"Nah. She's not my . . ."

"*Jaiden*!"

"Oh. I guess she is," I said. "I'll . . ."

"Go see what she wants?" Jenny said with a giggle.

"Yeah." I stood up. "Be right back."

"I'll read over the assignment," Jenny said. "Maybe we can get some work done."

"Sounds good," I said.

I liked her. Really. It wasn't like staring at her across class. She knew *South Park* and *Star Wars*.

But what the hell did Nancy want?

I scrambled down the stairs and realized we had company: two guys, one woman, all in dark suits. Nancy pointed to the tallest, the one with slick black hair.

"Jaiden," Nancy said. "This is Frank Gerard from Legal. They have . . ."

"Frank who from where?" I said, my voice cracking.

"I'm sorry," Nancy said. "They went over my head."

"We have a short waiver for your partner to sign," Frank Gerard from Legal said.

Part of me died. Then another part. Then another. I think a total of five parts of me upped and died. If I'd been a cat with nine lives, more than half of me would be dead.

"My partner? Jenny? Are you crazy? You'll ruin everything!" I was shouting in spite of myself, not even thinking she might hear.

Frank kept a steady voice. Lawyers, after all, are used to being yelled at. "The situation here creates the possibility of certain contingencies. It's our responsibility to ensure that should those contingencies occur, NECorp's exposure will be limited."

"Take your contingencies and shove them!" I shouted. "What about *my* exposure?"

"Jaiden!" Nancy said, sounding like a mother for the first time in her life. "Look, I'm sorry. I didn't know this would happen. I guess this was just a stupid idea."

She said something else to Frank Gerard, but I didn't hear it because I'd turned and was running back up the stairs. I raced into "my" room and slammed the door. Startled by the sound and the look on my face, Jenny jumped up.

"Jaiden, what's wrong?"

"Nothing! We . . . we have some company and my mom wants us to be quiet!"

I heard footsteps.

"Then why are you screaming? You look all red-faced."

Frank Gerard knocked. The doorknob turned.

"Jaiden?" Jenny said.

I threw myself at the door.

As I struggled to keep it shut, I smiled and said, "Jenny, think maybe you could leave through the window? It's really cool, and it's only a short jump to the sidewalk."

"Mr. Beale," Frank Gerard said. "You're only making things more difficult."

Jenny knew the deep male voice wasn't Nancy's.

"Who is that?" she said.

I wedged my shoulder into the door and pushed for all I was worth.

"It's okay, really. Just, maybe . . . the window?" I knew I wasn't making any sense.

"We just need a moment of the young lady's time . . . ," Frank Gerard was saying.

"Um . . . no one's here! It's fine, Jenny, really . . . they're just salesmen."

The hinges creaked. The door bent. Frank was stronger than he looked.

I flew forward, spun, and fell flat on my butt. Figuratively and literally.

The suits swarmed in, black blazers and attaché cases a blur.

Jenny stood up on the bed and looked like she was going to scream. Frank whipped out a pen and a three-page document with the NECorp logo on it. He handed it to Jenny, who looked more and more like a deer caught in headlights.

A very cute deer, mind you.

"Who are you?" she yelped.

"Attorneys. We just want to make it clear that while we're not saying the woman downstairs is *not* Jaiden Beale's mother, we're also not saying she *is*. It's a simple waiver, but I want to assure you that any protections you have as a visitor in this house and as a minor would be identical, legally, as if she were. That includes injury due to equipment malfunction, fire, or the unlikely event of unwanted sexual advances from Mr. Beale."

"Sexual advances?" Jenny shrieked.

"No! No! Will you shut up?" I screamed.

It was like a nightmare, only the monsters were really well dressed.

Jenny was looking back and forth between me and the suits. She looked like she was going to freak any second and run away. I'm not one for praying, but I sure did then.

The woman in the blue suit finally found her voice. I thought maybe she was going to try and calm Jenny down, but instead she cleared her throat and said, "Jennifer, you . . . uh . . . will have to get a parent to cosign since you are a minor."

You can guess what happened next, right? Exactly.

Jenny freaked and ran away.

5

ACTIONING OUT

The front door slammed, and I dove for the window. I wanted to throw it open and scream something, but couldn't figure out what. Instead, I watched Jenny race off on her bike. Her hair flashed in the sun as her body and the bike got smaller and smaller until she was a dot, and I couldn't tell which part of the dot was Jenny, and which was her bike.

Funny how one minute you can feel like you're on top of the world and the next like you're under it.

The suits and I stayed in the room. While they looked at their watches and made a few calls, I kept myself busy by making small moaning noises.

I don't know why they stayed. Maybe they were so stupid, they figured Jenny was coming back with a parent to sign the freaking form. Or maybe they figured the people they worked for were so stupid that they should look like they were waiting for her, in case someone really, really stupid asked them about it later.

I think that second one was most likely.

Common sense or boredom soon won out, and they left. I sat pathetically on the bed, cradling my Falcon model, remembering how Jenny liked it.

Ten minutes later, Nancy came by and stood in the open door. She looked like she wanted to say something, but, like me at the window, couldn't figure out what it was. I sure as hell wasn't going to start the conversation for her.

After just standing there got too ridiculous, she shrugged, said: "Take an hour to pull yourself together. I'll see you back at the office," and left.

At least she looked a little sad for me.

So there I was, all alone, in my crappy fake room, in my crappy fake house, with my whole crappy fake life. I thought about smashing the Falcon just to smash something, but Jenny liked it. I thought about kicking in a door. These were cheap, hollow, and couldn't block any sound, let alone stand up to a good kick. After running through a long list of things and people I really wanted to smash, I couldn't think of anything that would make me feel better that wouldn't lead to something that'd make me feel worse.

Because if I really smashed anything, Team Jaiden would just get me into a behavior modification program or send me off with some accountants, or maybe some doctor would put me on drugs for my ADD or bipolarism or depression or whatever it is they're calling being alive and feeling royally screwed these days.

And that did it. I mean, really.

You ever have a moment when you suddenly realize the thing you want most out of life, the thing you've been working hardest for, kind of even counting on in the back of your mind, just ain't gonna happen, no way, no how?

I want to say it wasn't about Jenny, but it was. Things were working out like I couldn't believe, and fate just yanked her out of my hands. And by fate, I guess I mean the legal department of NECorp, which is a lot like fate, if you think about fate as something powerful that you can't escape. Kind of like the aliens in the Alien movies, without the dripping slime.

And lawyers *never* die.

So why bother wanting anything anymore? Sure, there were still some DVDs I hadn't seen, and I still had some levels to go on Doom VI, but that wasn't exactly something to pin a life plan on. When you're done with a DVD or a video game, you can think about the best parts for a while but even that starts to get dull sooner or later.

But a crush, now that'll never bore you. Not me, anyway. And when Jenny left, I felt like I wasn't allowed to even have the crush anymore, and, man, if you can't have a private little feeling in the back of your head, what can you have?

So, I ran away.

Ben once told me I ran away when I was six, because I hated my tutor. I made it all the way to the boiler room, but I never even thought to leave the building. NECorp's headquarters was the world to me.

I don't remember that, but I don't have any reason not to believe it. When you're a little kid, you think running away is heading down the block with a knapsack full of cookies. You figure you'll meet a hobbit or a flying horse and come back in time for dinner with everyone so happy to see you they'll serve ice cream instead of veggies.

I wasn't looking for treats anymore. I put on my hoodie, got on my bike, and rode off, thinking I wasn't going to come back unless they shot me with a tranquilizer dart.

It had warmed up since morning, turned into one of those autumn days where the temperature was just right and there were big clouds in the sky that looked like the billowy cotton from a Q-tips ad. A few people were mowing lawns, doing gardening. Little kids played in some of the yards. As I biked past them, I felt like everyone was staring at me. Maybe because they'd never seen me in the neighborhood before. Well, they weren't going to be seeing me again.

At the end of the road, about where Jenny vanished, I hit an intersection. To the right, it led onto an access road for the expressway that connected the corporate parks to the main bridge that headed north, where most of the ers came from. I don't know what I was thinking, that big roads lead to bigger places, but I followed it.

In no way was I allowed to bike anywhere near the expressway, so this was already a major revolution. I was breaking rules, crossing boundaries, feeling free. Nancy and Team Jaiden would probably call this a paradigm shift—if only because they insist on taking the fun out of everything.

I stuck to the shoulder and tried not to wobble, but even here the cars zoomed by at forty or fifty miles an hour. It was dangerous as hell, in my mind anyway, the chief advantage being that every time I heard an engine rumble—my mind was not on Jenny so much as on staying alive.

I kept this up for a couple of miles, then swerved off toward a familiar street sign: Gunson Road. I'd never noticed before, but once you get past that development where the fake house was, past all the bright and shiny corporate headquarters, things get gray and grimy. The houses get older, and are more packed together and painted less often. Most of them held more than one family.

I was a little surprised. The reason I'd swerved off was that Ben lived around here somewhere. If I changed my mind I could try to drop in on him, but I never pictured him living in a rundown area. I always figured Ben was secretly well-off and was just a short-order cook because he loved flipping eggs. I also didn't remember the name of his street, and the looks of some of the side streets didn't make me feel like exploring.

So yeah, okay, I pedaled a little faster, but I tried to look cool about it. Finally, I reached a huge avenue with strip malls and gas stations. I got off my bike and walked it across the four lanes. I had a little cash on me, in case I'd wanted to go get something with Jenny. Now I planned to hit a CVS and get some running-away supplies. You know, cookies, milk, and maybe some sugar for my flying horse.

Seriously, by this time, I had a plan. I'd buy blankets and enough food to last me a few days, go into the woods, stay until the heat died down, then come out the other side, near the interstate, and try to make my way across state lines. After that, maybe I could work odd jobs as I traveled across the country. You know, like the Hulk.

Have I mentioned I'm a fan?

I knew I'd have time before Team Jaiden was hip that I'd flown the coop. Nancy had left me alone because she knew I needed some "cooling down" time. It'd probably be two hours before she'd even start to wonder about me. When she finally came looking, there were lots of places I could be—the gym, the cafeteria, my room—it'd be at least another hour before she exhausted those.

That's exactly how she'd play it, even if she did get worried. She was methodical—not like my last manager, "Smiling" Al Jensen. He wanted to put one of those ankle bracelets on me so my location could be tracked. Can you believe it? Like I was a criminal.

We didn't get along so well.

Anyway, the strip mall parking lot was like an asphalt desert, huge and flat and cracked. Even though this was Saturday, the place was pretty empty. Maybe it was because I was feeling particularly alone, but seeing it gave a whole new meaning to the word *desolate*. You could see dead weeds in the cracks, and I'm talking thick weeds, like if you pulled one out and hit someone with it hard enough, you could do some damage.

I was wheeling my bike along when I noticed four kids hanging out near this lame fast-food place, Herbert's Burgers. They were leaning on the only car near the place, and it looked as bad as the parking lot; full of dents and cracks and a couple of half-hearted patches of that red stuff they paint over rust with.

As for the kids, they didn't look dangerous. They were just, you know, kids. They were older than me, maybe by a few years. A couple wore blue Herbert's Burgers vests, so I figured they were just taking a break from work. As I got closer, though, I could see they were kind of tense. Really quiet and stiff, and nobody smiling.

I wasn't scared or anything, not yet anyway, but I found myself watching them. This was partly because they were the only sign of life around, and partly because there was a girl with them and she looked . . . interesting.

Her skin was pale, practically white, her eyes a quarter

of the way closed—I guess you could call them bedroom eyes. She wore a tight white T-shirt and these hip-huggers cut well below the navel, which made me start to understand our school's dress code. If the girls at Deever dressed like that, I'd never hear a single word a teacher said. Her front teeth were kind of funny, though, not quite buck teeth but getting there, and one of them looked chipped.

So here I was, running away, looking at the way this girl was dressed, and damned if I didn't feel like I was some kind of outlaw. I even smiled at her. She smiled back. It was pretty cool.

There were three guys with her, but I don't really feel like describing them, except to say one was tall and thin with that really, really awful acne that seems to replace major chunks of your face with this rubbery pink crap, another was kind of fat with glasses, and the last guy had big muscles and a mean look in his eyes. I didn't know any of them from Deever. They all looked more the sort who'd dropped out of high school, which would explain the Herbert's Burgers vests. The tall, thin acne guy looked really unhappy, like he'd just seen a mirror or something.

I was thinking, Hey none of my business, I should just take my smile and keep moving. So that's what I tried to do. But as I started to wheel my bike away, acne guy took the cigarette he was smoking out of his mouth, put his arm way up, and chucked the burning butt down on the ground like he was mad at it. Then he stomped on it with his foot. I mean, stomped. First one foot, then the other, then both. He was wearing these really old sneakers, torn a bit on the sides, and he stomped so hard they looked like they'd rip apart.

When he was done, he ripped off his Herbert's vest, threw that on the ground, and stomped on it, too. While he was doing all this, he shouted a word over and over, a word which I don't think I should repeat. I'm not going to say "freak," "frick," or "frag" or something lame like that, but you can guess what it was.

All grumbly, he lit up another cigarette, picked up the now-dirty vest, and put it back on.

So, yeah, I was staring.

And, yeah, maybe I had an expression on my face that showed how crazy I thought he was. So, of course he noticed me, and of course he didn't like the fact that this little geek with a bike was staring at him.

He jutted his acne-covered face forward and kept it out there, pointed at me like a gun.

"What?" he said, real nasty. I don't know if his voice was low and gravelly like that, or if he was just lowering it to add to the effect.

I shrugged, trying to keep cool, but honestly, I was getting scared. He was bigger and older than me, had a bunch of friends, and there was nowhere I could run.

I tried looking confused as if I didn't know why he was talking to me at all, even though I knew exactly why he was. I think it's some sort of animal instinct: when faced with a threat, you pretend you don't know what's going on.

"Leave him alone," the girl said. "It's not his fault you got sacked."

Really pissed now, he looked at the sky like he had a personal relationship with it, and said, "Great. Does the whole world have to know?"

Well, that's not exactly what he said. He stuck that magic word (that rhymes with stuck!) in there three or four times. Then he started stomping around again, punching the air, spitting, cursing, like he was going to turn into the Hulk.

The heavy one nodded toward my wheels as if none of this was going on. He had on these square glasses and wore denim pants. His head was really round and squat, like a pumpkin. You know how glasses make some people look smart? Not this guy.

"Bike broken?" he said. He talked fast, so at first I thought he was speaking in a foreign language—*Bayuk böken?* Luckily, before a huge amount of time passed, my brain managed to play it back slowly enough for me to figure out what he was saying.

"No," I said. "I'm just tired of riding."

He nodded. I think maybe he was trying to be friendly, to make up for the other guy's lousy attitude.

No one said anything else, so I turned and started walking. After a few paces, I felt stupid for being scared. The guy had just gotten fired, and compared to some execs I've seen get the axe, was handling it pretty well. I mean I've seen those guys dragged off kicking and screaming by two or three security guards.

So I said, "Sorry you got sacked."

Bad move. I guess an older guy getting pity from some stupid kid with a bike was embarrassing.

"What do you know about it?" he shouted. He looked so pissed, I backed up like he was going to bite me. He stepped toward me, maybe figuring I'd be as easy to stomp on as the vest, and he wouldn't have to wear me afterwards.

I'd like to say he was going to get his butt kicked. After all, he was thin as a scarecrow and I'd taken all these self-defense courses, but I'd never been in a fight, and all of a sudden I forgot everything. So, really, I was the one with the ass about to be kicked.

That is, until the girl with the hip-huggers shouted "Ranker!" like she was yelling at a bad dog. He responded like a dog, too, furrowing his brow, lowering his shoulders, and panting.

She, meanwhile, looked at me, mortified. "I'm sorry. He's my brother. There's something wrong with him. He's not good with people."

I started to say, "It's okay," but Ranker shook his head.

"Nothing wrong with *me*," he said. "People, people suck. Stupid people. People."

He kept saying "people" like someone invisible was using his voice to scratch-jam, so it was easy to see what his sister meant. There really was something wrong with him. And his expression wasn't as angry as his voice. It was dull, what they call robotic, and his eyes, like his sister's, were partly closed. Only on him, it didn't look sexy.

It was pretty creepy.

"Ranker," she commanded, "say you're sorry."

Ranker stopped moving and looked at his feet.

"Sue!" he said, but Sue glared at him like she was going to smack him with a rolled up newspaper.

He said "sorry" to his sneakers, like he was apologizing to them for letting them get so ratty, but then he looked at me, said "sorry" again, and looked away real quick.

Then the heavy guy with the glasses started talking.

"He worked six months, fifty hours a week for seven bucks an hour, and they fire him. No notice. May, the new girl they hired last week? She makes assistant manager."

I had no idea what it meant to earn seven dollars an hour. I had no idea what it was like to earn anything. Team Jaiden has me on an allowance, so I save for DVDs or games sometimes, but that's about it. Still, I figured from the way the heavy guy said it that it wasn't very much.

Thinking back, this was another opportunity for me to just nod and go back to my whole running-away thing, but at the time that seemed rude, so instead I said, "Really? That sucks. Why?"

Ranker glanced up at me, then looked away again. "Because May smiles. She looks people right in the eye and says, 'Can I help you?' like she really believes she's helping, like it makes her a good person to serve 'hamburgers' and 'fries' and 'salads' with 'ranch dressing.' "

He said it without making the quotes with his fingers the way some people do, but you could hear them, like every word in quotes was something he hated with all his guts.

"She even knew the names of the regulars and remembered what they ordered. I didn't even know there *were* regulars."

Ranker reminded me of Georgia, this woman who used to work the front desk at NECorp. She scowled constantly, so they canned her. Now there's Bernadette, who smiles so much you want to puke. I preferred Georgia. With her, you knew where you stood, and if she ever did smile, you could believe it. Bernadette, who knows what she's thinking? Could be a psycho killer.

Still, I was thinking I could give poor Ranker a few pointers.

"Remembering people is just a trick," I said. "You pick something weird that reminds you of them, like if you think Mr. Smith has a nose like a cucumber, picture his face with a cucumber on it. And for the smile, well, can't you just force yourself to smile? That's supposed to work."

It was true. During "Smiling" Al's brief tenure, I had to sit in on a couple of Customer Relations lectures where they explained the smiling thing. Apparently, if you smile a lot, you actually feel better. It's like your hormones and stuff that cause your moods decide that if you're going to look happy, you may as well feel happy.

But Ranker shook his shaggy head. "Can't do it. I tried, but I always look down. I can't even to talk to someone long enough to find out what their name is."

"What happens when you try to smile?" I asked.

"I can't. I just can't. Get it?"

"Why should he? Why should he have to smile?" the third guy, the bruiser said.

So they don't fire you, I was about to say. But I felt funny, like I was missing the point, and they were all bigger than I was.

"I told you," Sue cut in. "There's something wrong with him. He can't read people's feelings. It makes him short-circuit."

"That's for sure." the heavy guy said.

It dawned on me that Ranker's pals were kind of like Team Jaiden, with sister Sue taking Nancy's part. The heavy guy was Jack Minger, trying to make people feel better, and Muscle Man was Bob, just repeating what everyone else said in different words as if it made some kind of difference. Which I think meant that Ranker was me.

"Gotta be myself. Gotta be myself," he said to himself. "But I need the money. Need the money . . ."

Sue walked up to him and tried to calm him down, but

he kept pulling away.

"Gotta be myself, but I need the money . . ."

It was kind of like one of those really short poems. A haiku? Only, I'm sure it didn't have the right number of syllables.

Now that everyone was getting so familiar in a really bad sort of way, I decided I really should get going. I'd taken a few steps away and was just starting to pick up steam when Sue screamed "Ranker!"

I looked back in time to see Ranker running full tilt on those long, lanky legs of his, toward Herbert's Burgers. Sue and the other two were running after him. He was fast though, and rounded the corner to the front of Herbert's before they could catch him. They followed right along and disappeared inside.

I stood there, staring, thinking, well, this can't be good. What was Ranker going to do? Punch out the manager who fired him and get arrested? Punch out May and get arrested? Would May still be smiling when they hauled her into the ambulance?

Clearly I should have kept going, but it was kind of like watching a car wreck. From where I stood, the only thing I could make out was half a brick wall, so I took a few steps closer, trying to get a view of what was going on inside.

By the time I could see through the window, Ranker, Sue, and their two friends were already running out, even faster than they ran in. And speaking of smiling? All four had goofy grins on their faces. Ranker held something big in his hands, but I couldn't make out what it was. It couldn't have been too heavy, because it wasn't slowing him down much.

Sue was screaming, "Run! Run! Run!" as she laughed.

When Ranker saw me, he headed my way. Around then I noticed what was in his hands.

It was Herbert.

Actually, it was one of the plastic statues that sits on the counters of all Herbert's Burgers. Ugliest damn thing. The franchise founder, who may or may not have been named Herbert, apparently hadn't heard about branding, because he kept the same stupid design he started with back when he couldn't afford to pay for one. It looked like a five-year-old made it. It was this guy, with no neck and a spatula, wearing what I guess was supposed to be a chef's outfit, only his white hat was shaped more like a fire chief's hat.

Ranker ran at me, carrying this two-foot statue. And me, like a total idiot, stood there long enough for him to shove it into my arms. There I was, staring into these two grotesque, off-size eyes as Ranker, Sue, and their pals zipped past me.

Then someone else ran out of the restaurant. At first I thought he was a manager, then I realized Herbert's Burgers managers don't generally pack sidearms. It was a policeman. Running. At me. And this wasn't one of those donut-eating, overweight types. He was young, fit, and fast.

The smart thing would have been to say, "Hey, officer, I had nothing to do with this. Here, take Herbert, return him home. I hope he doesn't suffer any trauma." But of course that's not what I did.

Can you guess what I did do?

That's right. I freaked and ran.

6

RUNNING UP THE FLAGPOLE

"Hold it!" the police officer shouted. He didn't sound unfriendly, just demanding.

But I didn't listen, I just kept running, cradling Herbert. You might think this is a pretty radical move for a kid raised by a corporation who has never been in trouble with the law, but really, it had nothing to do with that. The thing is, when someone's running after you, running is a very natural thing, almost like not smiling when you have to stand behind a cash register all day. I think it's part of what they call the flight or fight instinct.

Team Ranker dove into their crappy car. They were still laughing, but the cheery sound was fading, like it was dawning on them, as a group, that maybe it wasn't so funny. They fired the engine up, tires squealing against cracked asphalt, the car fishtailing as they headed for the road.

You'd think any police officer worth his salt would give up on me, get into his car, and go after the real crooks, but not this guy. As they peeled out, he did one of those quick stops, where your feet hop side to side to slow you down. But then he picked up speed again and kept chasing me. Why? Probably because I was holding the statue, his first priority being to retrieve the kidnap victim.

This didn't dawn on me for about twenty yards. I was too busy running and being a little pleased that all the time I'd spent in the gym was paying off. I won't kid you. I wasn't losing him, but he wasn't gaining either. I heard him talking into his cell phone, or radio, calling in about the speeding car, and that probably slowed him down a bit.

About this time, I started realizing it was the statue he wanted, not me. Which meant, if I dropped it, he'd leave me alone, right? The only problem—how to drop it? I couldn't slow down, exactly, or he'd have me, so I sort of lowered it and let it tumble out of my arms, down to the asphalt.

Bad move.

CRACK!

I don't think you could make a cheaper statue if you tried. It shattered like an egg full of plaster. Herbert-chunks and Herbert-dust flew everywhere.

With Herbert now a big white splotch on the asphalt, the cop kept chasing me.

Like I said, this was a big wide space without any-place to hide. I wasn't worried he was going to shoot at me, not much, anyway, but if he had decided, hey, I'm going to put a cap in this kid's ass, he would've have had a nice clear shot.

A row of stores was coming up. Most were open, but I could just picture what would happen if I dove into one. Everyone inside would turn to look at the crazy guy bursting through the doors. Even if I did find a place to hide, they'd probably just all point at it when the cop came in.

A chain-link fence ran along the edge of the parking lot and disappeared behind the stores, so I headed for that. Beyond it were the woods, the place I was planning to run and hide anyway. If I could make it into the woods, I might be able to lose the cop.

Lose the cop—now I was thinking like an outlaw. That's a long way from ordering my breakfast with the home fries just how I like them. Part of me figured, well, that's the deal if you want to be your own man in these mean streets. Mean parking lot, anyway. The other part of me, the cold and scared part, remembered exactly how good those home fries tasted.

On the lighter side, I wasn't thinking about Jenny very much. Except maybe about how if I got caught and she saw my picture on the front page of the paper, I would die. Because, you know, that's where it'd be. *Teen Inc.*, *Juvenile Delinq* or something like that. So, okay, yeah, maybe that thought made me run a little faster.

The backs of the stores had floodlights that shone on the fence, but past the fence, where the woods started, it was like a dark wall had been put up. Now I had to get over the fence.

The actual climbing wouldn't be a problem, but the top was covered with coiled barbed wire, which made me wonder what it was keeping out. Raccoons, maybe, that might get at the trash, but what raccoons needed barbed wire to stop them?

Fortunately, I'd seen enough escape scenes to know what to do. As I ran, I yanked off my hoodie. With it in one hand, I climbed the fence. At the top, I used it to cover the barbed wire. Cool, huh? Some may call us film geeks, but there's actually useful information to be had in medialand.

Climbing over the sweatshirt was slow, and I was only about halfway over when the cop appeared. I was on the edge, about to drop into that darkness when he saw me. He did another of those tap-dancing stops and shouted, "Get down from there, now!"

I froze. This was kind of it. I could still let him catch me, call it a day, and go back and face the music. After all, I hadn't done anything wrong. Except for the running. But would that matter? Wouldn't I still get in the papers?

A light shone on my hand. He'd pulled out a flashlight from his belt (those guys are equipped like Batman).

"Give it up. Guy last week climbed over one of those things and sliced his leg so badly they had to amputate," he said. "Don't be stupid."

I didn't believe him. They can sew whole legs back on.

How could a cut make you lose your leg? He was playing me for an idiot. Which made sense, since who else but an idiot kid would be running around with a stolen statue of Herbert? Still, I felt insulted.

I wasn't sure what I was going to do. I like to think I was really going to run for it, but I slipped and tumbled, down into the dark, on the wetland side. I felt my arm catch one of the razor wires. There was a pinch, followed by an almost painless slicing feeling, then another pinch. A second later, I was more worried about the ankle I'd landed on, which felt twisted, and the leaves and twigs I was eating.

The cop came running up. My back was to him as he shone the light through the fence links. "You all right in there?"

He sounded concerned, so I answered. "I hurt my ankle and I think I cut my arm."

Actually, I knew I'd cut my arm. It was hurting more and more. When I touched it, I felt wet blood through the torn sleeve.

The cop eyed the fence. You could tell from his face there was no way he was going to try to climb it.

"Wait right there. I'll find a way over," he said.

The second he was gone, I stood up, slipping a little on the wet leaves. When I put pressure on my ankle, it started beating like it had its own heart. Worse, I felt a stream of blood running down my arm, across the back of my hand, and along one of my fingers.

I may have been in shock. My whole body went into robot mode, like it could only remember the last command from my brain, which was, run. So I stumbled on.

After a few yards, I heard what at first I thought was leaves rustling in the wind, but it wasn't windy. Then I realized leaves didn't gurgle. There was running water out in the dark somewhere. As I took a few more wincing steps, my eyes began to adjust. A half moon rose in a clear sky, giving off enough of that freaky blue light for me to make out the edges of trees, the ground, and water.

It was a concrete drainage ditch. I knew it ran alongside the expressway then turned off deeper into the woods. I got closer to the water's edge, thinking I could stick my ankle in, soothe the swelling, maybe even wash my cut. But it looked dirty, like liquid silver in the moonlight. You could see a little layer of oil or grease swirling on the top.

I could see the blood on my arm now, too. It looked black, which was cool, though I was too scared to think so at the time. I pulled my shirt down over my shoulder and shimmied my arm free. There was liquid black everywhere. So I climbed on top of the concrete, and balanced on some of the rocks at the water's edge.

I either put too much weight on my ankle or hit a slick spot. Next thing I knew, I was in the water, freezing. It felt like being all wet and in a meat locker at the same time. The water wasn't so deep that I couldn't stand, but the current was very strong, so every time I took a step toward the bank, I was pushed farther downstream.

My ankle stopped throbbing and just plain started hurting. I could see that the cut on my arm wasn't too bad. It was about three inches long, still weeping blood, but the cold water seemed to slow that down. It stung, though, worse than iodine. And the water didn't just feel cold, it felt like it looked, oily, like something not water.

I wasn't thinking too much about it. Mostly I was busy getting knocked down by the current. When I hit a deep section, I sucked water into my lungs. I was off my feet, trying to keep my head up, coughing. It was hard to tell how far I'd gone or where I was. I couldn't see the fence or the stores. The water stung my eyes so much I had to close them.

With a thud and a clunk, I hit something hard and metal, and stopped moving. I grabbed at it with my good arm. Water ran from my hair down into my eyes, but I forced them open and made out that I'd hit some sort of rusty grate built into a concrete bridge. I held on and tried to pull myself up, but it wasn't going that well.

Then I felt something on my arm, grabbing me, pulling me.

I thought for a second maybe it was one of the mutant raccoons, that they'd take me to their underground city and make me their king. But it was a human hand, a strong hand. The policeman, I figured, but no, I looked up into a familiar face.

Ben.

Short-order cook supreme. He looked all freaky blue from the moonlight, but it was definitely Ben. He was pulling at me with both arms now, and I dropped the raccoon fantasy and started thinking instead that the whole thing was a dream, that I'd wake up back in bed. It would still be morning and my date with Jenny wouldn't be ruined.

Only the pain in my ankle, and my arm, which was getting worse, felt real. So did the cold as Ben rolled me onto the dirt and leaves.

I asked him the obvious question. "What're you doing here?"

He gave me a look that said, "Shouldn't I be asking you that?" but instead he said, "Nancy's been calling everyone including the army. I thought you might head this way, so I was driving around when I saw your bike in the lot. Then I saw that cop come running around the other side of the fence."

He rubbed his thumb against his index finger and noticed I'd bled on him. "That's not good. Let's get you out of here."

I thought he'd lift me, but we're the same height, so instead he helped me to my feet. I figured I was headed for a police car, but the cop was nowhere in sight. Ben was watching for him, too, which made me realize he wasn't going to turn me in.

I saw the fence looming. "No way can I climb that again," I said.

Ben got this little smile. "You won't have to."

As we reached it, he turned, put his back to it and pushed. The chain-link spread open behind him in a line and he pulled both of us through. Okay, so for half a second I thought it was magic, but really, there was just a tear in the fence that I hadn't seen.

We walked up a hill and there was his pickup truck. My bike was in the back.

Moving fast, Ben pulled a T-shirt from his gym bag and wiped my arm with it. "Don't worry, it's clean," he said.

He looked at the wound the way a mechanic might look beneath the hood of a car. "You might need stitches. We'd better get you to a hospital."

He wrapped the shirt around the cut and told me to hold it tight. He didn't have to, I already knew that part. Then we hopped in the truck and headed out, driving right past two police cars coming into the lot. It was great, like in the movies, only with twice the adrenaline.

Once we were down the road, I exhaled and asked him, "How'd you find that hole in the fence? That was lucky."

Without taking his eyes off the road, he reached down and held up a pair of wire cutters. "Sometimes you make your own luck."

"Ha!" I said. "That is so cool."

He glared at me. "No, it's not cool, Jaiden. And don't think that's the end of it."

He flipped open his cell phone and pressed a number on speed dial.

"I've got him, Nancy. You can start breathing again."

"Aw, no! Did you have to?" I said, slumping sideways into the seat. I should have expected it, but part of me was hoping we'd both go on a crime spree or something.

"He's got a sprained ankle and a pretty deep cut. I'm taking him to the emergency room," he said. His brow furrowed as he listened. Ben has these thick eyebrows, and when his brow furrows the hairs in the center rise up like little antennae.

"What? But . . . but . . . Fine." He snapped the cell shut.

"What?" I asked.

"We're going to my house. They're sending a car. With their own doctor."

"And there's something wrong with that?"

He looked at me, then back at the road.

"I had half a mind to let the cop take you. It'd teach you something."

After the way he said it would "teach" me something, I didn't feel so grateful anymore. I thought about trying to explain, but instead I clammed up.

His house wasn't far. Apartment, I mean. Two rooms on the third floor of a three-family house off Gunson, with barely enough property for the driveway and the garage. By the time you walked inside his apartment, you were in the middle of the biggest room.

It was clean, though, and there was lots of cooking stuff in the kitchen, neatly organized, like it was a store. There were weights in one corner and photos of a woman on the wall, maybe his wife or ex-wife, but I didn't ask. It sure didn't look like there was enough room for two people in the place. I was feeling crowded just standing there.

Ben stood there. I thought maybe he was embarrassed, but I realized he was just trying to figure out what to do while we were waiting. He sat me down, took the T-shirt off, and looked at the cut again.

"Bleeding's stopped. That's good. But I don't like that color."

I twisted my arm to see. It ached, not on the cut anymore, but beneath it. The skin at the edge of the tear was greenish.

"What is that?" I asked.

Ben shrugged. "Don't know. Maybe you're just still cold. Cold skin turns colors. Blue usually. I'm sure the doctor will figure it out." Then he made a face. "You know that was stupid, right?"

I shrugged.

He looked me dead in the eyes. "What happened with your friend stunk, but you've got to understand, your whole life you've been inside NECorp. It's like a fish tank. Everyone can watch you, but you're safe. School is one thing, but you just don't have enough experience with the world to try running off like that."

I looked at him, annoyed. I felt guilty about being annoyed since he'd rescued me and all, but I was annoyed just the same.

"So what are you saying? I'm too lame to make it in the world?"

All of a sudden he didn't sound like my main man anymore. He sounded like one of the suits.

"No, you're making it out all wrong. Ever hear of the bird in the gilded cage? It may want to be free, but if it got out, the first cat it ran across would have it for dinner. I know your life feels like a prison sentence, but keep getting yourself into situations you have no clue how to handle and you'll see exactly what the difference is between a corporation and a state penitentiary. You hang tight, though, four more years and you'll be done with NECorp. You can do whatever you want. You'll be a free man."

"Free?"

He shrugged. "Free as any man can be."

I wasn't sure how to respond, but as it turned out I didn't have to worry much. Out the window I could see a black limo pulling up. Nancy got out of the back.

My gilded cage had arrived.

Freedom, like Elvis, had left the building.

7

A WIN/LOSE SITUATION

Ever have an experience you think'll change your life, but all it does is stick you back where you started, only now you're more miserable because you're convinced things can never change? The rest of the night was like that, starting with Nancy being worried my bleeding would ruin the limo's leather interior.

And it got worse. If she was stiff and robotic before, now Nancy was like the Herbert statue, only without the goofy smile. I thought she'd at least show some relief that I wasn't dead. But she didn't. She just stared out the window, yellow streetlamps flashing on her face, her skin what they call ashen.

I was thinking of saying, "Sorry, Mom," to lighten the mood, but something told me not to. The only thing she said was, "The doctor will meet us at NECorp."

The ol' HQ never looked more like a mad scientist's castle than it did that night. It was ten, and almost all the interior lights were off, making the windows black, but the outside spotlights made the white walls glow.

Two sleepy security guards met us at the door. They flanked me and Nancy as we all marched through the huge lobby, past a big, ugly abstract sculpture that cost millions of dollars, past the cafeteria to the infirmary.

Dr. Gespot, one of three doctors who looked after me, was waiting, tired and annoyed. He not only stunk of cigarettes, he was also what they call morbidly obese.

I know people have all sorts of body types, and if someone starves themselves to look like a pencil, that's weird, too. I think Nancy, for instance, is a bit on the thin side. But I always thought it was particularly weird to meet a doctor who smoked, or was really huge, since he should know exactly how that affected his health.

Gespot's weight also made his exams very uncomfortable. When he tried to listen to your heart, his gut would push at your side. Bet he never got an accurate reading because of that. Having that big chunk of gut press into you *had* to raise your pulse.

Luckily, he was just looking at my ankle and arm. First, though, he snapped on some latex gloves. "Protects us both," he once said, a comment that made me wonder if he had something.

He twisted the ankle and I surprised myself, since I usually don't scream that loud.

"You've got a bad sprain." He said "you" like he was

talking to me, but really he was talking to himself and maybe a little to Nancy, who was busy punching data into her Blackberry. "We'll x-ray it just to make sure."

Not every corporate facility has its own X-ray machine, but NECorp's did, thanks to me. They were concerned about any bad press about my health getting out.

Next, Gespot tried to peel Ben's shirt off the wound. Some blood was already dry, so the cloth clung to the cut. With a little tugging it came free. He swabbed the edges with cotton and sprayed some stuff on it. For a second it felt soothing, but as the stuff got under the skin, the length of the cut ached.

He looked at it, really curious, like if I was paranoid I'd say, "What? Am I going to die?" Then he pushed at it a little with his latex-covered finger. Under the examining room lights you could see that the green around the edges really was strange.

"How long ago did you get this cut?"

"Hour and a half?"

"What did you cut yourself on?"

"Barbed wire."

He looked at me like I must be lying, but Nancy confirmed it with a nod.

"That's pretty fast for an infection to get this bad, but I suppose it can happen. I'm going to give you a round of antibiotics. And you'll need a couple of stitches."

I thought about those mutant raccoons and wondered

if I'd been infected with their blood. Maybe during the next full moon, I'd be one of them.

"Unless he develops a fever, he should be able to go back to school Monday." He paused. "*Will* he be going back to school?"

Nancy's brow furrowed. "Haven't decided."

That surprised me. I thought I'd be locked up until I was eighteen. "You mean you *might* send me back?"

"The decision hasn't been made. We'll discuss it Monday morning."

School. For the first time, it dawned on me I might have to go back to Deever and see Jenny.

Gespot injected some other stuff to numb me up, then it was just like sewing. You feel the pinch of the needle, and the thread sliding in and out, but as long as you don't get freaked out by what it looks like, it doesn't hurt.

Once I was patched up, Nancy walked me back to good old Area 2B and introduced me to this guy standing outside who looked like a college-aged tank with curly black hair. Not someone I'd mess with, which, I guess, was the point. This was Anthony, a new security guard who'd now be posted directly outside my office suite.

He smiled, all friendly, as if to say "We're going to be buddies." I was too intimidated not to smile back.

"Eight A.M. Monday," Nancy said. Then she left. She hadn't even called me by name all night. I didn't know if she was disappointed, hurt, scared, all of the above, or *none* of the above.

82

As I got undressed I was thinking I was too upset to sleep, but when I hit the pillow, I went right out. No dreams, no nothing. I just remember opening my eyes, seeing a dull glow lining the blinds and realizing it was morning.

Sunday consisted of waiting for Monday. I watched some DVDs, played some games, but couldn't concentrate. It was raining to boot, so everything outside the window looked as gray as everything inside me felt.

My arm still hurt, but it takes days for antibiotics to kick in. No fever to keep me out of school, unfortunately. I wanted to peek under the bandages and see if the wound was still that funny color, but Gespot had told me to leave it alone.

My personal security-bot, Tony, turned out to be not such a bad guy. He was studying to be a marine biologist, thought the corporate nine-to-five life sucked, and didn't blame me for running away. Not that he was going to let me out of his sight. But we got along. Played some tournament-style Doom. I rallied for that and kicked his butt, because you can't just let someone beat you in Doom. That made me feel a little better.

My food was brought up on trays and Tony took it in to me. That was it for the day. Something about the possibility that I might have to go to Deever made me tired, so again, when I climbed into bed I swear I'd just closed my eyes when my alarm clock went off.

I didn't bother to wash. I just pulled on some clothes

and met Tony in the hall. I was thinking maybe we could do a perp-walk kind of thing, but he didn't have any hand-cuffs. I was tired and embarrassed, so I didn't say good morning to anyone. Tony almost got lost a couple of times and I tried to direct him to the right conference room. He looked at me like maybe I was trying to trick him, but eventually he believed me.

When we reached the door, I was disappointed to find out he'd wait outside. I was hoping to have him stand behind my chair, like he was my bodyguard. If anyone got out of line, I could have him shoot them. Then again, the guy didn't even have a gun.

Walking in, I noticed three extra chairs, expensive chairs, at the table. Instead of one of those boxes of coffee-to-go and paper cups, there was a carafe and ceramic mugs. That meant one thing: Super-Creep Veeps. They don't drink from paper, unless they're trying to act like one of the guys, and they don't like to do that often, probably figuring what the hell is the point of being a senior vice president if you have to act like one of the guys?

I figured on Jeremy Banks, from Legal, Carl Kracik, from Human Resources, and the new guy, Ted Bungrin, a trans-fer from NECorp's LiteSpring subsidiary, which made, you guessed it, lightbulbs, mostly fluorescents.

I hadn't met Ted, but everyone was all excited about him. He was what they all called a real "mover and shaker," which really just means he made things happen, which was pretty rare in the corporate world. Ben probably did more moving and shaking when he made scrambled eggs than any of these guys did in their entire lives.

To be totally fair? A year ago, Bungrin spearheaded a new manufacturing process using an innovative filter that reduced the amount of mercury waste the LiteSpring fluorescent plant produced by about 75 percent, while tripling output. Mercury pollution is a big deal, so that won NECorp all kinds of pats on the back, even an award of some kind from the EPA. Everyone felt good about it, and about Bungrin as a result.

As I walked in, Jack Minger, standing by the door, gave me a little smile. "You're in for it now," he whispered. His tone was joking, and I guess he was trying to be nice, but it didn't make me feel better.

I kept my head down as I walked to my seat, trying not to look at anyone else, trying to pretend they weren't all staring at me, studying my every move. When you look down as you walk, aside from the carpet, which was this gross burgundy color, all you see are shoes, pants, and occasionally legs. Everyone at NECorp is pretty well dressed, it's part of what they call the corporate culture, which isn't really a culture the way ancient China was, or Greece; it's more about dress codes and smiling at people you don't know or like.

So all the shoes and pants were new and clean and well pressed, but then I passed these real shiny black shoes that looked like they were coated in glass. Above them were these perfectly pleated gray pants that had to be tailor-made.

I couldn't help but look up.

For a second, I was staring at this chiseled face with bright blue eyes and perfectly trimmed black hair. The hair must have been fake or dyed, because the skin was a bit on the old side. Ted Bungrin. Had to be. Partly, because I didn't recognize him, and partly because he just looked like someone who moved and shook.

He nodded at me, not friendly or angry, just sort of in robot-acknowledgment. I kind of half-nodded back and slumped the rest of the way to my seat where I stared sullenly at the tabletop until Nancy said, "good morning," very loudly.

She looked unhappy. I expected that. But she also looked nervous, I guess because of all the big brass around. As everyone took their ceramic mugs to their seats, she kept talking. "Thank you for coming in so early. As you know, we had a very eventful weekend."

I looked around the table. All of Team Jaiden looked very guilty and sheepish, particularly Jack and Bob, except for Nancy. Her face was too brittle to look sheepish. I said she looked nervous, but really she just acted nervous, moving her head back and forth a few times too many. Her face looked mostly rigid and pissed, really pissed.

I hadn't noticed it before but there was also something

on the table in front of her, next to her laptop, and it wasn't a ceramic mug. When I realized what it was I had, as they say, a cow.

It was a plastic bag, which is no big deal in and of itself, but inside the bag, all covered with dirt smudges and barbed-wire tears, was my hoodie, the one I'd cleverly used to get over the fence and then not-so-cleverly left behind.

I closed my eyes and rubbed my head. Oh crap. Was I going to be arrested? I knew whatever NECorp would do to punish me would be a pain—more restrictions, less screen time, the usual—but if there was a police case and the press got wind of it, the whole fricking world would know who I was and what happened last night. Including everyone at Deever.

Including Nate and Jenny.

I felt nauseous, I really did. Ben was right. What made me think I could ever survive outside this place?

Nancy clicked open her laptop.

"I'd like to begin . . . ," she said, but then there was another surprise.

Bungrin cut her off, just by clearing his throat.

Having seen how much being cut off annoyed her, I expected her face to register something, but she just clammed up.

"What's the situation with the police?" he said. Nothing else, just like that. Even Super-Creep Veeps usually said "Excuse me."

Nancy opened her mouth to answer, but she was cut off (again!) when Banks from Legal spoke up. Jeremy Banks is an older guy who plays things laid back, like he'd been through so much that nothing could ever rattle him again. Despite his calm, cheery exterior, everyone at NECorp was terrified of him, even the other Creeps. I half-expected Banks to give Bungrin a lecture on manners, or at least let him know how we did things here at HQ, but he didn't.

Instead, he glanced pleasantly through his reading glasses at his Palm Pilot screen and said, with a chuckle, "Petty crime isn't my forte, Ted, but I think we have a handle on things. Restitution was made to the owner of the Herbert's Burgers in the amount of $112,365 dollars and no charges will be pressed. As a result of the excellent relations we've maintained with the local police, they've been very cooperative, mostly concerned about the safety of the boy."

I was too busy exhaling to care much about who was interrupting who anymore. No jail time sounded good. But six figures for that statue? The thing exploded when you dropped it, for pity's sake. Still, you've got to figure some of that is "personal damages," meaning hush money.

"Jeremy, was he identified? Do the police realize who he is?" Kracik asked. I don't think he really gave a damn, he just wanted people to know he was paying attention. "That could be a problem."

Nancy looked like she wanted to answer, but couldn't.

"No, Carl," Banks answered. "As far as they know, the boy's my nephew. Of course, I neglected to mention that I don't have any brothers or sisters, but Jaiden here feels like family to me," he said, again with a chuckle.

Everyone in the room laughed lightly, because they had to.

But Bungrin even cut off the laughter. He was a cutter, it seemed. Maybe that's how he moved and shook. Cutting, after all, makes you more efficient. "Okay. Good," he said. "Then we don't have to bother Desmond with any of this. That leaves us with the school issue. It might be wiser to switch him back to tutors for the time being. Limiting his exposure limits ours."

"I think that's for the best," Carl said, nodding like he was deeply impressed by the way Bungrin thought.

"No!" I shouted.

I said it like a little kid, loud and annoyed, and I grimaced right after. As for why I said it, it suddenly dawned on me that even though facing Jenny again would be awful, school was the only time I ever left this place. I'd go nuts if I couldn't go to Deever.

Everyone turned to look at me. Bungrin looked like he was confused by the fact that I knew how to talk. "You ran away. You vandalized a fast-food restaurant."

His sharp blue eyes were hypnotic, like a vampire lord's. I looked down at the table, real fast, before he could sap all of my will. I had to say something, no matter how lame, no matter how much it made me sound like some helpless, whining kid.

"I didn't vandalize anything. Some other kids, disgruntled employees, dumped the statue in my hands and ran off. Just let me go back to school. Please. I won't run away again."

I thought at least he might be tickled by my use of the phrase "disgruntled employees," but I didn't hear any pity in his voice. "You're right. You won't run away again because . . ."

"Ted, is this necessary?"

I looked up, shocked. Everyone did. It was Nancy, cutting Bungrin off. "He ran away because Legal screwed up his first date. Take him out of school, cut off his outlets, and you'll only be giving him more reasons to run away, or worse, become a candidate for medication."

Bungrin stared at Nancy. For about seven seconds, you could hear a pin drop, which is a really long time for a silence in the middle of a conversation. Everyone was holding their breath trying to guess what Bungrin would do. I was thinking laser beams from his eyes that would reduce poor Nancy to a pile of dust.

Instead he smacked his lips and shook his finger at her, which was just as good in a way. "Nancy, right?" but he wasn't asking, and he didn't wait for an answer. "We'll do it your way."

Whoa. No one expected that.

And with that, the Creep session was over. Bungrin looked at his watch and turned to his fellow alien masters. "Working breakfast, gentlemen?"

Kracik and Banks rose and followed Bungrin.

Everyone in the room, even me, exhaled all at once.

Bob headed over to the coffee carafe. "I bet Banks did have brothers and sisters. I bet he ate them," he said. Everyone laughed, really laughed, not like the pretend chuckling over Banks's crappy joke.

Jack Minger was beside himself. "Nancy! Going up against the Bungrin-meister! I didn't think you had the guts."

"Right," she said. "I'll send you my contact info at my new job."

I was feeling so good about her myself that I just said, "Nancy, thanks so much. That was great."

I'd hoped it was a moment for a reconciliation, but she just glared at me. Her mouth was the only part of her body that moved when she spoke. "You know, Jaiden, you're not the only one who gets hurt when you pull a stunt like this. Ted Bungrin wants to make some cuts, and he let me have my way just now, but if anything else goes wrong with you, it's entirely my fault. We could, seriously, all get fired."

Everyone at the table looked up, surprised, their expressions saying, "Really?" Then they all looked at me, pissed.

Nancy crossed her arms. "You are going to go back to school this morning, but Anthony's going with you."

I bolted to my feet. "On the bus?"

She shook her head. "No. No more bus. He'll drive you."

My voice jumped an octave. "And what then? Is he going to be handcuffed to me? Do I tell people he's my new Siamese twin?"

"I made the calls this morning. He's a volunteer at Deever's library. He'll be assisting in some of your classes, and keeping an eye on you. No one has to know why he's really there."

"No way!"

"Yes. No complaints, Jaiden, not one, or it's back to the tutors," Nancy said. She slammed down her hands on the table in this first-time-ever show of emotion. It was like she was taking out all her frustration with Bungrin on me. Between yesterday and today I'd had enough.

I started shouting at her. "Don't give me that. You screw up and you know what happens? You get replaced, but *I'm* still here." I stood up. I knew everyone was watching me, but I just kept staring at Nancy. "You know why you're letting me go back to school? It's got nothing to do with what's good for me. It's like you said. You just know if you don't, I'll run away again, or I'll go to the press and tell everyone what a freaking prison this place is!"

I expected to get slammed, punished, or at least yelled at, but I didn't. It was a weird moment that got weirder when Jack said, softly, "You wouldn't really go to the press, Jaiden. Would you?"

I stared at him, open-mouthed. It occurred to me for the first time in my life that they were afraid of what *I* might do to *them*. That *I* had the power to get *them* fired.

Nancy just glared. I could see her thinking, strategizing, unable to come up with anything in response. "It's late," she said. "Go to school, Jaiden."

"Fine," I said.

I stormed out. On the way I grabbed the plastic bag with my hoodie.

Tony had already eaten, so he went back to my room to get my books, while I got on line for a quick breakfast.

"So it goes," Ben said when he saw me.

"So it goes," I repeated. It was from a book I read for that science fiction thing in Mr. Banyon's class, and one of Ben's favorites, *Slaughterhouse Five* by Kurt Vonnegut. It was something we said when things were pretty bad.

"Arm okay?" he said as he cracked my eggs.

I nodded.

"They letting you stay in school?"

I nodded again.

He smiled a little. "Good. Good. So, the SVPs aren't always so stupid."

I shook my head. "It wasn't them. It was Nancy."

As he flipped the eggs, Ben raised his eyes, impressed. "Good for her."

I made a face and twisted my head. "Yeah, well, I yelled at her anyway."

He scooped the eggs onto a plate with the home fries and set it on the counter. Before I could take them, he pointed at me with his spatula. It was long and flat and had bits of potato and onion clinging to it. "That was stupid. You need to know who's on your side here, Jaiden, and you need to be good to them. Not everyone is, you know."

I shook my head. "What's that supposed to mean? They all have to be nice to me, don't they? It's their job."

Before I could say anything else, Ted Bungrin, the "cutter," walked right to the front of the line, passing me and the six people standing behind me.

And then he took my plate.

"I'm in a big hurry," he said sort of to himself. "Mind if I grab these?"

I could tell Ben was annoyed, but Bungrin just looked at him, that bemused smile on his face.

"All yours, Ted," I said, pushing the plate toward him.

Bungrin stared at Ben another second, then took off with the plate.

"Son of a bitch," Ben said to his back.

"Hey, it's okay. Tony's driving me to school. I don't have to catch the bus," I said, but Ben just kept glaring as Bungrin took the plate to his table.

"Hey," I said a little louder. "I've got to be good to the people who're watching out for me, right?"

Ben looked at me. The right side of his lips crinkled into a smile, but his brow was angry. When he went back to glaring at Bungrin, even the smile vanished.

I had to ask him twice to cook me some more eggs.

8

WINNING PEOPLE AND INFLUENCING FRIENDS

A few years ago this cutthroat corporate strategy guide came out called *Bob's Big Book of Business*, or—the 4Bs. At first it was published by, you guessed it, a guy named Bob, who was in his thirties but unemployed and living with his parents. The book hit number one on Amazon and Bob got totally rich and famous. Mr. Hammond liked it so much that everyone at NECorp, from Ben to the Creep Veeps, got a free copy.

That was before Enron, a big scandal I never understood and don't particularly want to. After that, everyone hated the 4Bs, calling it a symptom of the worst side of corporate greed. I don't know whether that meant everyone at NECorp had to give their free copy back or whether they just kept it out of sight, like the dirty pictures I know some of them watch online, but I do know I was unlucky enough to have "Smiling" Al Jensen make me read the whole awful thing when I was twelve.

Anyway, the 4Bs had all this mumbo jumbo about kill-or-be-killed strategies. The book was written in short sentences with a beautiful layout, for folks with short attention spans (or "little free reading time" like it says on the cover) so it should have been easy, but man, it just hurt. Reading that book was more boring than sitting and watching grass grow.

Despite that, and I hate to admit this, when I'm faced with tough situations, its boldfaced, large-print sayings sometimes pop into my head. Not because I find them a useful guide to life—more because they're a surefire way of knowing what not to do. For instance, there's this section about maintaining balance and dignity in the face of loss, which I think in psychiatry they call denial. The 4Bs says there's nothing wrong with pretending that whatever went bad was either somebody else's fault, or it never really happened, or that it really happened in a way that makes you look good.

I never bought into that. Me, I figure the only way to deal with losing is to throw yourself on the mercy of your enemies. Which is just what I did when I went to talk to Nancy about Tony, before I left for school that morning. You should have seen me, it was pathetic. I was writhing like a slug covered in salt. I begged, I pleaded, I whined, and I swore up, down, and sideways I wouldn't try anything. I wouldn't breathe, I wouldn't think, I would love her like Big Brother if she just cut me a little slack and didn't make my return to school any worse than what it already had to be—the worst day of my life.

It worked, I guess. We reached a compromise, which the 4Bs defines as something from which no one walks away happy, but everyone can live with. In this case it may have been right.

So, even though I wasn't allowed on the bus, after parking his car a few blocks away, "Eyeballs" Tony hung back twenty paces as I walked toward Deever High. That way, I could pretend I was on my own.

Which, I guess, was just another lie anyway.

With Eyeballs behind me, I walked up and put my hand on the overpainted door's cold silver handle, and just stood there a moment, staring at the bumpy patterns that thick, butt-ugly paint made, like it was a painting by Vincent Van Gogh.

It wasn't a big spiritual moment, I was just scared. In my heart of hearts, I just knew Jenny had spread the word all over school about what happened back at my "house." The second I walked in, I expected everyone to stare at me in awe and disgust like I was the Boy in the Bubble or the Two-Headed Armless Wonder or some other lame freak.

Tony waited, letting me have my door moment, like it was even obvious to him what a wreck I was. Nice guy. I figured if I was right and everyone did stare at me, I'd handle it for about five seconds, then ask him to shoot me.

"Hey, man, really, it's okay," I could tell him. "I love Big Brother."

But before I went in, a few kids walked past me and didn't even stop to stare. I thought for a second they might be the only ones who hadn't heard, but what were the odds? So, I pulled open the door and let the warm weird smells of Deever wash over my face while my eyes adjusted to the slightly green tint of the fluorescent lights.

There, in front of me, was the hall, the school, the kids, the teachers, all just doing what they usually did, standing, chatting, you know, what they call "milling." No one gave me a second glance. I even waved hello to a couple of people who ignored me.

Just didn't see me, I figured.

It was kind of disappointing.

I guess I'm all about the drama. The only reaction I got was from Nate. He, at least, came chugging up to me like an express train, wearing these baggy black jeans he thought were cool but just looked like they didn't fit. Grinning, he slapped me on the back like I was his dead brother returning from the grave.

"Jai-den! My man! You never called! How was the big date? Tell, tell, tell!"

Big date?

That stopped me short. I felt like I'd entered a time warp. I guess I had, in a way. Nate didn't have a clue about the whole end of the world thing that happened over the weekend. As far as he was concerned, my life was still in Friday afternoon, poised on the edge of greatness. To this man, to this friend, I had not yet fallen from grace.

And how did I repay his concern, his camaraderie, his caring? I said, and I quote, "It was . . . umm . . . tell you later, okay?"

Like that would work.

"No, dude, now!" he demanded.

I shook my head. He grabbed me by the shoulders and started shouting. Now people *were* staring. "You bastard! You're like the first man to walk on Mars and you're refusing to talk?"

Out of the corner of my eye, I caught a glimpse of Eyeballs bristling at Nate's enthusiasm, so I gave my man a little shake of the head, to indicate he was not a real threat and there would be no need to put a cap in his ass.

"Lunch," I said, but I said it kind of neutral, like maybe it meant I'd tell him everything at lunch, since we had lunch the same period on Monday, or maybe out of the blue I just sort of felt like saying the word, *lunch*. That way, later, he couldn't exactly call me a liar.

Nate shrunk a little, disappointed. I felt bad. But then his eyes narrowed. "Why weren't you on the bus?"

"My alarm clock's busted. I got a ride."

Lame. According to the 4Bs, the second lie always is. It says you don't get really warmed up until the third or fourth. Nate didn't notice anything weird about what I was saying, he was too busy noticing the bandage on my arm with its dollop of dark red still seeping through the cotton.

"Wicked," he said.

I smiled, thinking here was an opportunity to use my own strategy, hiding in plain sight. "I cut it on a rusty fence while a cop was chasing me," I said.

"Yeah, right," Nate said,

His head twisted. "So how *did* it go?"

"I fell into a river and got away."

"Not the fantasy, stupid. Saturday. Jenny. Project Hook-up."

I looked at the clock like it was later than it was and said, "Lunch" again in that noncommittal tone of voice.

"Are you kidding me? Tell me, right now . . . unless . . . you messed it up, didn't you? You totally messed it up."

Here at least I allowed myself a little genuine honesty. "Pretty much," I said, nodding.

Nate scrunched his mouth into a small *O* then asked, "So, what'd you do? Try to grope her or something?"

I shook my head, relieved to be annoyed at him. "No! What about you? You ever use Caitlin's chat-room handle now that you've had it forever?"

He grabbed his heart and made his classic face-of-pain.

"Touché, mein freunde," he said, stumbling backward. "Touché."

The bell rang. He started walking backward down the hall. "I still want details. You owe me details. At lunch."

He disappeared into the "milling" crowd, leaving me feeling like I'd hurt him somehow. I should have told him. He's my best friend after all, and Nancy was right when she said it wasn't going to be a secret forever. Nate was just warped enough to think it was cool, anyway. But the 4Bs was ringing in my head: *If No One Knows About It, It Isn't Real.*

And I didn't want any of it to be real.

As I walked to homeroom, I came up with more lies, like an explanation for Tony, in case Nate or someone saw me driving home with him: *He's my long lost half-brother. He had amnesia after a car accident and just remembered who he was.*

Smooth, huh? I was becoming a great little 4B follower. I was even stupid enough to think for a minute or two that maybe Jenny wouldn't remember what had happened, that somehow it would still be Friday for her, too.

But it wasn't. And there's no Santa Claus or Easter Bunny, I hear, either. At least that's what the memo said. Matt Bolton, my Team Leader before "Smiling" Al, never had the guts to tell me face-to-face. It's not my joke but Matt was what they call a "seagull manager"—he flies in, makes a lot of noise, craps on everything, then flies out.

Ironically, I believe he was fired via memo.

I continued to bask in the illusion of a normal day. In homeroom, the teacher didn't make any announcements about me. She just took attendance and sent us on our merry way. I nodded at Tony as I passed him in the hall and he gave me a discreet thumbs-up.

Math was my first class, then ancient history, so I thought I had a couple of hours of daydreaming to look forward to before Jenny and biology, but I was wrong about that, too. No sooner did I turn a corner, than I walked into her. We literally bumped foreheads. Her hair kind of flew forward into my face and I caught a whiff of fruity-smelling shampoo. Either that or she was eating one of those watermelon candies again.

We both took a step back. I got a good look at her, thinking I should take it all in, because it might be my last chance to see her without hearing how she hated me. Looking down as I rubbed my head, I could see she was wearing capris and a pink shirt. The capris showed off her calves, which kind of made me dizzy on top of the rush of fear. Then I looked up at her pretty face, surprised to see how tired she looked.

"Oh," she said.

"Oh," I said back. Then I threw in a terrified, "hi."

"Hi."

Practically at the same time, we both said, "Are you okay?" Which I guess would have been adorable, if my throat hadn't felt like it was crammed with pebbles and sand.

Then she said it. "You're the kid who was adopted by NECorp thirteen years ago, aren't you?"

I felt like I swallowed all the pebbles and they were sitting in my stomach. I felt like you'd have to put more clothes on me before I could even feel naked.

"How'd you guess?" I asked. Realizing how stupid this was, I followed up with, "Was it all the lawyers at the house, or did you just Google my name?"

She shrugged. "Both. There were a lot of baby pictures of you, then after about age five, nothing."

"People got bored with it, I guess." I looked down the hall. Tony was pretending to hang some poster or something. I looked back at Jenny.

"Did you tell anyone?"

She shook her head. "No. I'm not *that* uncool. But anyone can Google you. You didn't even change your name. It's not tough to figure out. What made you think you could keep it secret?"

"Because you'll only figure it out if you're looking, and before today, no one had a reason to look. It's called hiding in plain sight."

"You could've just told me."

"I *could* have?"

"Well, no, probably not. I don't think my dad would like it very much. But I'm sorry I freaked. It was so lame of me to run out. I just wasn't expecting, you know . . . lawyers."

Looking back, I should have paid more attention to that crack about her dad, but I was deeply distracted by the fact that *she* was actually apologizing to *me*.

"And . . . and . . . I'm sorry . . . that I *am* a freak."

That was an opening, see? I wanted her to say something like, "Oh Jaiden, you're not a freak."

But she didn't, instead she said, "Jaiden, it's not your fault."

Could have been worse. At least she didn't say, "Jaiden, it's not your fault you're a freak." That would have really sucked.

By now my heart was racing and my brain was zipping off in all sorts of directions. Mostly, I wanted to know if Jenny was really okay with me being who I am, or if this was just like one of those formal apologies and she'd also be sorry that she never wanted to be seen with me again.

The most clever way of finding out was, of course, by asking:

"So . . . what do you want to do about the bio project?"

"I could tell Ms. Chrob who you are and ask for another partner on the grounds that it's too freaky."

My eyes went wide. "Please . . . don't."

She looked at me like I was crazy then giggled. "Of course I won't! I'm sorry. I was just kidding."

Then, playfully, she punched me in the arm. Right in the bandage.

"Ow!" I said. Because, you know, it hurt.

She did a girly gasp and put her hand to her mouth. "Oh! I'm so sorry! I didn't see the bandage!"

Right. How could she miss it? It was like a quarter of

the length of my arm and had that dollop of blood on it. Then, out of nowhere, she started rubbing it with her hand and saying, "Sorry, sorry, sorry. Are you okay?"

Which made me think maybe she just hit it so she'd have an excuse to touch me. I can dream, can't I?

I gave her a combination of a smile and a frown that I imagine made me look kind of cute. "So . . . still partners?"

Still smiling, she nodded. "Yeah, but next time let's meet at my house. Tomorrow after school?"

I wanted her to say it again a couple of times. Not because I hadn't heard her, just because I liked the way it sounded.

"Sounds good," I said. Feeling daring, I poked her on the shoulder. "I'll have my people call your people."

It took her a few seconds before she got the joke, but then she flashed a smile and whirled away.

She knew I was watching her, because as she walked down the hall, she stuck her hand up and waved backward at me. That's the kind of thing I'd never try in a million years, because if there wasn't someone standing there watching you wave, you'd look pretty stupid. So she knew.

As she passed Eyeballs, he looked at me and gave me another thumbs-up. It wasn't even first period and the guy was already a pain.

I was late for class, but as soon as it ended, I headed into the bathroom and flipped open my cell to call Nancy.

You're not allowed to use cell phones in the school except in an emergency. I think by emergency they mean if someone's choking to death or some kids are shooting up the halls with rifles. For me, this counted, too.

"This better not be about Anthony," she said.

"It's not. And again, I am so sorry about the way I talked to you at the last meeting, but Jenny wants me to go to her house tomorrow to work on the bio project."

"That's great, Jaiden," Nancy said. She actually sounded pleased.

I got to the point of the call: "Anthony. Can't. Come."

"Jaiden, wait . . ."

"No. No way is Tony coming. Look, I know you've got your job to worry about here, but there's got to be something else we can do. Can't you just find one of those collars you can put around my ankle so you can track me by computer?"

There was silence for a while, then, "I don't know if it's legal, but I'll look into it."

The line went dead. I clamped my hand into a fist and said, "Yes!"

Of course then I started wondering if the collar would be small enough to hide under the cuff of my pants.

It took forever to slog through second period, but bio was heaven. I got there early, sat right behind Jenny, and talked with her before class started. I think even the stuff Chrob was talking about may have been interesting, but I might have just been in a good mood. The next two periods were another slog, but then it was lunch.

"What are you smiling about?" Nate said, throwing a fry at me. Deever cafeteria fries are soggy and heavy, not crisp and light like the ones at NECorp, so they don't throw very well. It just sort of flopped onto the linoleum at my feet. "I thought you completely screwed up things with Jenny."

"I was totally wrong," I said, sliding into the seat opposite him with my tray. I flicked a cheesy pasta elbow at him with my spork. Sporks give you much better accuracy and speed than a free throw. It landed in his hair near his right ear. Clearly, I was in the zone. "Things are going great. I'm going to her house tomorrow."

"It's the Jade-master!" Nate beamed.

"Nate, you know those bracelets they put around your ankle if you're a prisoner, so they can track you?"

"Yeah?" he said, swatting the piece of macaroni out of his hair.

"How big are those things exactly?"

Yeah, yeah, I didn't tell him about NECorp or about running away and the cops, but by now I was figuring I would later on. I mean, here I was thinking my life was all over, and now everything was working out great.

At the time, I didn't realize this was all just the calm before the storm and *Bob's Big Book of Business* wasn't going to help me whether I did what it said, or not.

I was going to be on my own.

9

BACK IN THE BLACK
AND BLUE

As it turned out, I didn't have to worry about a tracking device. Nancy assured me they could track me through my cell phone. I knew this was possible, there are even Web sites that do it for you, but I wasn't sure if she knew that. Either way, I wasn't going to mess with her, not after she was being so gracious.

See, in an effort to bolster her case with Bungrin, she spent the afternoon reading some book about adolescence for idiots that said we needed freedom, but with limits, or we'd explode and become Goth-killer drug addicts. That was enough for her to stick, or maybe cling, to her theory that NECorp's interference in my social life caused me to run away in the first place. If things were going fine with Jenny, I'd have a reason to stay. Don't fix it if it's not broken, right? So, she took it upon herself to let me sail solo.

After school Tuesday, Eyeballs just drove off in his

inconspicuous car, and I was all of a sudden free again. Or, as Ben had said, free as a man can be.

But there I was, walking with Jenny. It was a great fall day, with a nice crisp wind blowing dried leaves all over the place. We took turns trying to stomp them out of mid-air, making them crunch beneath our sneakers. Jenny almost fell once and I had to catch her. Well, she probably wasn't really falling and I probably didn't really have to catch her, but it was still nice.

Bumping shoulders, we walked through the field in back of the school, then out among the big suburban houses in the development. It all made the parking lot at the shopping center feel like another world, the weekend like a bad dream.

Then, out of nowhere, she asked, "So what's it like being raised by a corporation?"

I wanted to say something intelligent. I thought about using my prepared speech for the eventual television interview. But instead, I just said, "I don't know. What's it like to be raised by two parents?"

She looked a little disappointed, like she was trying to start an interesting conversation to get to know me better and I screwed it up.

"I know my parents love me. They raised me by choice. NECorp doesn't love you."

"No," I said, "but I love Big Brother."

And she thought *she* wasn't cool. I thought it would be

funny, but after I heard myself say it, I realized it was cryptic and weird. This was confirmed a second later when Jenny scrunched her face and said, "Huh?"

I rattled my brain and started kicking dead leaves.

"I'm still raised by people, really. Corporations are made up of people, aren't they?"

I never in a million years thought I'd be defending NECorp, but Nancy had just put her job on the line so I could be here with Jenny, and, well, it was okay for *me* to hassle them, they were my parent corporation, after all. But Jenny was still sort of a stranger.

She didn't take it well.

"The people don't matter. They just serve the corporation, and the corporation only exists to make a profit."

I stopped kicking leaves and looked at her. I mean, there are arguments on both sides, right?

"So they showed that documentary in your history class last week, too, huh?" I said.

"Come on, Jaiden, do any of those people really care about you like a family, or are you just like a product to them?"

I thought about Nancy and Bungrin, and Mr. Hammond. Then I thought about Ben.

"Both," I said. I'm not sure why her question made me incredibly antsy—I guess because it felt like she was implying there was something wrong with *me* because of how I was raised.

I left it like that for a while, but I wanted to say something intelligent, so, yeah, I dug up one of those answers I made up for my television interview, and, about a half block later, went into my little sound byte.

"Okay. It's like I'm living inside this machine, and, yeah, I'm just a product to it, but so's everyone else, because the machine can only see things as products. But there are people living with me inside the machine, and some of them care about me, and some of them know how to work the machine. I mean, it's not all that different. Everyone's a product in some way, right? It's just that that's not all we are."

She seemed surprised. And she didn't say anything. I felt embarrassed about making such a weird speech, so I never asked what she thought.

By then we were at this yard that was so totally covered with leaves you couldn't see the front walk, like whoever owned the house didn't even have a rake. I'm not used to lawns being a mess like that, everything at HQ is manicured by a huge staff, so I made a face at it, and I guess Jenny saw it, because, surprise, surprise, it was her house.

Perfect. Things were going just great.

"Dad likes to mulch them with the mower, but he gets so wrapped up in his work this time of year he forgets to mow," she said.

I didn't really care, it just surprised me. As for her dad, I didn't know if he worked so hard because they needed money, or because he loved what he did or because he was one of those type A workaholics, like Nancy.

So I asked: "What's your dad do?"

Innocent question, yes? Fit right in with the flow of the conversation, didn't it? Only, Jenny didn't answer. She started walking really quickly up the hidden walk.

"He's working at home today," she said. She said it the same way I'd said "lunch" to Nate earlier. As I walked up behind her, she stopped in her tracks and put her hand on my chest to stop me. It was very effective.

"Jaiden, don't mention anything about NECorp to my dad, okay?"

"Sure! I was just about to ask you the same thing."

She nodded. "Good."

Then she opened the door.

The house itself wasn't very different from NECorp's corporate rental place. It pretty much had the same center-hall floor plan. What was different was the decor. I mean I expected it to look less like a hotel, which it did, but I didn't expect it to have such a . . . well, you know how some houses have a color scheme, and if you're really anal, everything, even the furniture and the napkins, match? This place didn't have a color scheme so much as a theme, and if I had to give it a name, it would be *anticorporate*.

It wasn't really subtle either, like as soon as you walked in you were facing a poster on the wall that read, Corporation = Death.

No, really. It gets better. Jenny pulled off her coat real quick and pulled me deeper inside. The main hall and the living room were likewise plastered with slogans:

People, Not Profits

Soulless Corporation Is Redundant

Down with the Group Mind

Enjoy Your Fascist Regime *(I kinda liked that one)*

Corporations: You Can't Live with Them and You Can Live
  Without Them

There were tons of books and papers all over the place, too, and little pieces of artwork scattered here and there: a hand crushing a bar code, a painting of some businessmen posing with Ku Klux Klan members, an American flag that had images of corporate logos instead of the fifty stars, and a huge list of things to boycott, from Apex Cola to Zaggut Crunch bars.

There was even a small bust of Che Guevara. He was an Argentinean revolutionary and sort of the poster boy for the far left. He was executed by the repressive government of Bolivia, because, well, he was trying to overturn it.

I mean, I really had to wonder where they did their shopping. Probably not Wal-Mart, huh?

Now, you've got to understand, I know it's important, but I really don't care a lot about this stuff. Politics has never been a natural draw, not when there's a new video game or a DVD around. Yeah, my peculiar upbringing has made me a little more aware of things, like all that glop from the 4Bs, so I sort of knew what I was looking at here. Jenny's dad was one of those people who detested capitalism. In other words, he was what the Creep Veeps would refer to as a Communist.

Here's the nearest I can figure things. From what I'd read about the big-time Communists like in the old Soviet Union or Communist China, they want to create a perfect world where everybody gets what they need and does what they can, only they kill and repress a lot of people in the process. Many religious fanatics try to create perfect worlds and wind up killing and repressing a lot of people in the process, too, so I always figured they had a lot in common. Yeah, I know, corporations do that, but they don't pretend so much that they know what's best for all humanity the way Communists and religious fanatics do. Call them pigs or whatever, but they really do just want to make money, and if it turns out to be more profitable *not* to kill a lot of people, well, they won't.

Don't get me wrong—I'm not saying it's better to kill a million people for a profit than it is for an idea. It's more like I think not killing anyone could be a great and highly profitable idea.

Anyway, when I saw all this stuff up on the walls I had a kind of knee-jerk reaction, just like I did to Jenny's comments. It was like someone had a poster up saying my parents were the enemy.

I didn't say anything for a bit, I just looked around, taking it all in. Jenny was standing right next to me the whole time. She had a sort of chagrined look on her face and was waiting for my reaction.

"Oh," was all I could manage.

Then this older guy came up to us wearing this ratty, rough-looking brown sweater over a T-shirt and some green army pants. He had stubble that seemed to cover all his visible skin, including his face and hands, and wore thick black glasses that matched his curly hair. His face was thin and his skin kind of hung funny on it, and he moved around quickly like a chipmunk. He rubbed his hands together as he maneuvered around boxes and papers on the floor, then, as he reached us, stuck one out to shake mine.

"Jaiden," he said. He smiled and nodded his head in quick little jerks. "Nice to meet you. You're working with Jenny. I'm Eric Tate."

It was only then that I realized he was Jenny's dad.

I grabbed his hand, shook it, and said, "Hi, Eric . . . ," because I call most everyone at NECorp by their first name. But then I felt funny about it and quickly changed it to, "Mr. Tate."

Jenny looked nervously around. I could tell she was trying hard not to stare at either of us.

"So," I said. "Nice house."

He looked around like Jenny had, as though he were

seeing it for the first time. "Yeah, we used to have a lot of paintings around before Jenny's mother died. She was a little more abstract than me. I like art to say something."

I turned to Jenny. "I didn't know your mother died. I'm sorry."

She shrugged and said softly, "It was a long time ago."

Mr. Tate rubbed his hands again. "Why don't you kids make yourself a snack in the kitchen and get to work. I've got a phone call in a few minutes. I'm being interviewed by the local paper."

Jenny brightened. "They're going to do an article? Finally?"

Mr. Tate smiled. "Maybe. It's just an interview right now."

"That's great!" Jenny said. She ran over and kissed him on the cheek. You could see how proud he was and how happy Jenny was, and so I guess I got a little caught up in that and started smiling myself.

"Congratulations," I said. "What's the article about?"

He looked up at me and grinned. "How NECorp is poisoning the local water tables. I've finally got someone to listen."

"Oh," I said, "but NECorp's not poisoning anything. They got an award from the EPA that . . ."

Jenny and her dad looked at me. He was still smiling, but she was making a face, like don't you dare tell him who you are.

"You know about the LiteSpring plant?" Mr. Tate asked.

I stammered a bit, but figured he could chalk that up to him being Jenny's dad and me being nervous. Finally I managed to say, "Yeah . . . I did a paper about it last year. They lowered the amount of mercury they use in their lightbulbs or something. The emissions went down 75 percent."

"That's what they say, yes, but I know different. It's fluorescent bulbs, by the way. Don't get me wrong—overall, fluorescents are great for the environment because they use so much less energy than incandescent bulbs, but they create light by shooting electricity through argon and mercury gas. Usually the pollution is a small issue. The thing is, according to my tests, ever since this new production process began at the factory a year ago, the mercury levels in the local water have steadily risen. They know about it, and they're trying to hide it."

I was about to say, *You don't know they're trying to hide it*, but I stopped myself.

I did get that weird you're-insulting-my-parents feeling again, but here I was, facing Jenny's dad, and he seemed so sure of himself. He was looking at me, pleasantly, but also sizing me up.

Jenny still had that "don't tell" look on her face, and I didn't want to blow it.

So I swallowed and asked, "Uh . . . how do you know they're trying to hide it?"

He seemed surprised I'd even question the possibility.

Then he took off his glasses, cleaned them with his sweater, and popped them back on, like he wanted a clearer look at me.

Much as he'd moved around like a chipmunk earlier, now he got totally steady and serious. "NECorp has a long, consistent history of negligence. In fact over the last three months, they've been spending a lot of time not answering my questions."

"Maybe you've been asking the wrong people?" I offered. I could put him in touch with Nancy, after all. Or Ben, he knew everything.

He twisted his head sideways, then looked at Jenny for a second before getting back to me. "Okay. Maybe. But ever since they started using these new proprietary mercury filters, every test I've done on the local water here shows increased levels of mercury. They're poisoning the water supply. They must know it, and they're trying to hide it. That fits my definition of evil. Doesn't it fit yours?"

I ignored the question.

"So . . . do you do water testing, like, professionally?" I asked. I guess I must have sounded aggressive or something, because he stiffened and sounded defensive as he answered.

"Yes, as a matter of fact, I do. I'm one of the founders of JenCare, a remediation company. We clean polluted sites. Testing the water and the soil and finding a way to clean it has been my job for about twenty years."

"Oh," I answered. "But . . ."

By then Jenny was grabbing my shoulder and yanking me toward the stairs. "We should get started, Dad. Big bio project to work on! Big, big, big."

Mr. Tate nodded, but kept looking at me. "Your mother, Nancy, works for NECorp, doesn't she?"

"*Now!* Gotta go, Dad." Jenny said again, pulling harder on me. This time, the phone rang.

"We'll talk again, Jaiden."

"Yes, sir," I said. For some reason, I added, "Good luck with your interview."

"Thanks," he said. "I intend to make as much trouble for them as I can."

He turned back to his study and Jenny nearly yanked me up the stairs.

"Phew!" she said loudly, as soon as the door was closed. "Not cool, huh?"

I shook my head. "No, not for me, not so much." I should have followed up by saying that I still thought *she* was cool, but I was rattled, so instead I said, "You could've told me."

"Told you what?"

"Well, that your dad's a Communist."

I was kind of kidding, but Jenny didn't take it that way.

"My father is not a Communist! He's trying to keep people from getting sick! Do you have any idea how poisonous mercury is?"

"Uh . . . no . . ."

She shook her head in a way that reminded me of her dad. I guess that's natural, what with people inheriting all kinds of traits from their parents. When you're looking at it close up like that, though, it's sort of supernatural, too, especially if you're seeing some angry middle-aged guy's face in the features of the girl you're trying to hook up with.

I'd been hoping we'd get back to that quiet moment before the lawyers broke in, that time we almost kissed. Now, listening to her, part of me was worried we'd be swapping spit and her dad's face would take over and he'd start screaming about how my saliva had mercury in it.

Turned out I didn't have to worry because after that, we didn't talk much at all. We actually worked on the stupid bio project for the rest of the afternoon.

We were definitely in major not-cool territory.

10

DOWN AND OUT SIZING

After Jenny's, I headed home, weirded out about what to make of Mr. Tate. He seemed to think I was just misguided, but if he found out *who* I was, he'd have a big cow over *what* I was. Not only that, but everyone at NECorp had been so proud of those new mercury filters, I couldn't believe it was a lie, even if Bungrin had been in charge.

But Mr. Tate'd probably point out NECorp was responsible for the faulty valve that killed my parents. Yeah, for that I hated them awhile, but after I toured the plants and the new managers explained how even with the mistake Dan Blake made it was totally unlikely that the one bad valve could slip through, I came to think of it as a fluke—like getting hit by lightning—and then NECorp got its ass kicked, right? I'm rich when I come of age.

Which only shows that while you can't put a price on human life, you can sure try.

But now, the thought that NECorp might be creating more mercury pollution, and that maybe they knew about it and weren't doing anything to stop it, was like, I don't know, maybe finding out that your parents are murderers.

Maybe they were evil, after all.

Not to be selfish, but what does that say about me? I was raised by NECorp. Was their evil in my blood? Was everything I read in the 4Bs encoded in my subconscious, waiting to activate when I reached a certain age, so that I'd turn into one of them? Had that been their plan all along, to brainwash me to give the money back?

I looked at my denim shirt cross-eyed, terrified it might morph into the smooth fabric of a business suit. I could almost feel the collar and tie materializing around my neck.

I needed someone to talk to, so I headed for the cafeteria to find Ben. Only, no one could tell me where he was. Figuring I'd see him in the morning, I went to my room, where things got even weirder.

There's a pile of stuff I keep carefully disarranged: comics, homework, game hint books. They were gone, swept aside, like they were garbage. Instead, there on the fake wood of my desk, centered and straight like an invader from Mars, was a white sheet of paper. Linen bond, too, not the cheap stuff, with a full-color, raised NECorp logo. It was from upper management. The Creep Veeps. What the hell did they want?

I clomped over, already pissed, when I glanced at my

computer screen and thought I was seeing double. There, on-screen, was the same memo. They were repeating themselves before I had a chance to hear them the first time.

The letter asked, ordered really, that I show up at a big meeting tomorrow. The CC field was a laundry list of all the Super-Creep Veeps. Bad enough, but it was the timing that really made my eyes bug out. Eleven-thirty A.M.—in the middle of my school day!

What were they thinking?

I speed-dialed Nancy. She didn't even say hello.

"It's not a mistake. It was the only time everyone could meet."

"Does that give them the right to just walk in here and . . . and . . . clean my room? What about school?"

"Jaiden, you're the only kid on the planet who'd get upset about missing half a day. You can be late once."

Yeah, only I wasn't about to announce that eleven-thirty put me past third period bio. Things may have been strained with Jenny, but I still wanted to see her.

"Is this about Tony not taking me home from school?"

There was a silence, one of those creepy ones that only lasts a few seconds, but seems to go on for years while the person at the other end tries to figure out what they should say. When it's quiet too long, whatever they do say is bound to sound like a lie.

"It's not that," Nancy said. "Everything isn't just about you, Jaiden."

"If it's not about me, why do I have to be there?"

More of that silence. So thick you could cut it.

"You'll see tomorrow. If I were you, I'd . . . I'd get some rest."

Her voice was hollow, like a computer voice that didn't have any inflection.

"Nancy, what's going on?"

Then it got really, really weird. She hung up. And all I had left was that silence. It stuck with me for hours, while I tried to beat my high score on Walking Killer Tank and got all the way through the special edition DVD of *Intergalactic Commandos*.

It was even still with me as I lay in bed, looking at the parking lot lights, counting the times the little green NECorp Security car swept the perimeter. The more I thought about it, the more my stomach tied into knots. I wasn't even worried about Mr. Tate anymore. Dads aren't supposed to like the guys their daughters date anyway.

Sleep was a nonstarter. I was biding my time until morning. The cafeteria opened at six A.M., and I was dying to see Ben. He'd tell me. I could even ask him about the mercury pollution thing and I was sure he'd know about that, too. I hopped out of bed at five-thirty, took up some time with a shower, then dressed and raced through the halls.

I made it to the cafeteria just as they were rolling up the gate. I ran up to the breakfast counter and stood there face-to-face . . .

125

. . . with some guy I'd never seen before. Ever.

He looked like an okay-enough guy. Big black moustache, hair bundled up under a net, thick arms, a little sweaty from the heat of the grill, but, a) like I said, I didn't know who the hell he was and, b) he wasn't Ben.

"What can I get ya?" he said, like it was the most normal thing in the world to ask.

"Where's Ben?"

His brow furrowed. I was afraid he was going to tell me he'd been working here for the last five years and had never heard of Ben. But he nodded.

"The guy who used to work here. He's in back."

By the time I said, "What do you mean, *used to*," I was past the counter and heading into the kitchen.

The place was full of steam and smelled more like cleaning fluid than food. Veggies were being chopped, meat sliced, fruit put in baskets. There must have been ten people, but no Ben.

The door to the locker room was open, so I went in and there he was. He was pulling stuff out of a locker and stuffing it into a bag. He didn't even see me until I said, "Ben?"

"Jaiden," he said, looking up.

"What's going on? What are you doing?"

He laughed a little. "What's going on is I've been fired. What I'm doing is packing."

Now I *knew* I was in the Twilight Zone. "Fired? Why?"

"Because I opened my big stupid mouth to the wrong guy at the wrong time."

"About what? To who? They can't fire you for just talking! I talk all the time."

He looked up. "You're not me. I'm an employee, so yeah, they can pretty much fire me whenever they want."

Done packing, he stood and faced me.

"Where are you going to go?"

"I have a sister out west I haven't seen in a few years. Cecilia. Says she'll be happy to put me up until I get on my feet again. Family's good for that."

"Yeah," I said, then my voice trailed off. "Family."

Ben twisted his head to catch my eye. "I'm going to tell you something, and I want you to listen carefully, okay? NECorp is not your family. You got that?"

I knew what he meant, but still . . . "Some of the people . . ."

"No," he said, real definite. "They may like you. They may even love you. But if they ever try to choose you over NECorp, they'll get the boot."

"Is that what happened to you?"

He shook his head, not like he was saying no, but like he wasn't about to explain it to me. "And forget what I said before about you being too protected to live out in the world. I forgot that sooner or later everyone lives in the world, whether they can or not. You had the right idea when you ran away."

I shrugged. "Except for the part with the police."

"Yeah, except for the part with the police." He headed for the door.

"But what do I do, Ben? Run away again? I'm here for another four years."

"Take care of Number One. Understand? Screw them. Doesn't matter whether you stay or go, but screw them. Just like they'd screw you."

I guess I understood what he was saying, but I'm damned if I could explain it. Then he walked out. And that was it. No explanation. No other advice, nothing. I didn't even have a chance to ask him about the mercury or the meeting.

I was alone in this stinky employee locker room, standing there like an idiot, staring at an empty locker until Mr. New Guy rapped on the wall to get my attention.

"You Jaiden?"

"Yeah."

"Uh . . . Ben . . . left something for you," New Guy said.

He handed me a plate with eggs, bacon, and home fries, just the way I liked them.

I was freaking, but I ate the breakfast. I didn't savor it, I just wolfed it all down. It wasn't Ben's best effort, but I figure he was as distracted making it as I was eating it.

If you think about it, anything can change anytime, like the way it changed for those people pushing their bagel carts in the Twin Towers when the planes hit. Everyone has expectations, I guess, like that the sun will rise or you'll have Ben's home fries every morning, or you'll live through the day. You'd go crazy if you thought you couldn't count on certain things, right?

So I spent the next hour going crazy.

When eleven A.M. came, I grabbed my backpack and headed to the fourth-floor executive meeting room, the only place Tony and NECorp would let me go anyway.

Usually I trot in like I own the place, but when I opened the door, I froze. The room was designed to intimidate, with a long, long table and a high, high ceiling. The chairs were huge, the way they're larger and more comfortable in first class than in coach. Even the air tasted pricier.

The rest of the room looked like the Valued Employee photo in the lobby. Anyone with NECorp mojo was here: Banks, Kracik, Jenkins from Acquisitions, Fogarty from Forecasting and Budgeting, Lewison from Marketing & PR, even a few guys from the West Coast office. They even all had assistants, Robo-Suits, men or women, but Robo-Suits just the same, standing stiff behind them, waiting for their buttons to be pushed.

The only one missing was Desmond Hammond III, which in itself was weird. Like maybe they were planning a birthday party for him. Or some other surprise.

At first I was relieved to see Nancy, but she looked so cowed. She didn't look up when I waved. I even said hi and got a big nothing.

Maybe this was about her letting me go to Jenny's without supervision? Were they firing her, too, like Ben? Was that what she meant about it not being about me?

Except for clicking laptop keys and shuffling papers, everything was terribly quiet. That is, until I hit the tile floor with my rubber-soled sneakers, which squeaked loud enough to shatter glass. Everyone looked up at me. Cowed Nancy winced.

I stopped dead, but what could I do? I'd make the noise wherever I walked in that room. Gritting my teeth, I headed toward an empty chair at the head of the table, squeaking madly all the way. I always sat at the head of the table, so I figured it would be the same here, but Ted Bungrin waved his hand and shook his head.

"That's Mr. Hammond's chair, kiddo. It stays empty. You sit there."

I glared at him, mostly because of the "kiddo," but he ignored that and raised the right side of his lips in a half smile, like he was saying, "Do I have to repeat myself?"

So, with my sneakers still squeaking, I dragged my embarrassed butt over to a seat next to Kracik. The chair creaked loudly as I pulled it out. And, of course, as if I hadn't been through enough, as I sat, the upholstery made this gargantuan farting noise.

Looking dead ahead at a wall, I'd no idea if everyone was staring, but if I were them, I would be.

Bungrin ended my comedy routine by speaking. "Nancy

requested we begin with Jaiden, so he can get to school, which I guess is more important than our schedules."

A few annoyed smirks lit the Creep Veeps' faces. Bungrin went on. "Point being our young ward was visiting Jennifer Tate yesterday afternoon."

Nancy spoke softly. "Yes."

Hearing that, I thought I'd figured out what was going on. I leaned forward in my chair, which made another loud fart, and spoke. "I know Nancy was supposed to keep an eye on me, and if you want Anthony following closer or something, I'm fine with that, but don't take it out on her, okay? Nancy's doing a top-notch job, really, much better than that last guy. And the whole running away thing, that was just . . . just . . ."

"Jaiden," Bungrin said, cutting me off. "We want you to keep seeing Jenny."

"What?"

For half a second I thought he was going to reveal he was actually an alien entity and I was going to be asked to participate in a bizarre breeding experiment.

"How was the date?" he asked.

Before that, his every word was quick and functional, so this was a change of pace.

"Did you meet her dad?"

All the Creep Veeps leaned forward. Even the Robo-Suits craned their necks. It was like they were all one big person with a lot of heads and eyes. Aliens.

"It wasn't a date," I muttered.

"Whatever it was, how was it? Did her dad say anything to you?"

Having read the 4Bs, I knew that what we were talking about wasn't what we were really talking about, but not knowing what we were really talking about, there didn't seem any harm in talking.

"We worked on our bio project."

"Great. Did you meet her dad?"

"Yeah . . ."

Bungrin shrugged. "What was he like?"

"He was . . . upset because he thinks LiteSpring is dumping cxtra mercury."

Jeremy Banks shook his head. "We knew that much."

Bungrin gave him a little wave of his hand that said, *shut up*. "Did he mention what he was planning to do about it?"

"Well, he finally got the local papers to listen and he had an interview with them."

When I said that, there was this gasp and all their heads moved back a bit. I looked at all of them as they stared at me, clinging to my every word.

Finally, it dawned on me what this meeting was about, and why I was there.

"You're worried about Mr. Tate, and you want me to spy. That's it, isn't it?"

Bungrin shook his head. "Spy is a comic-book word. It's

about TV and movies and heroes and villains. You're more sophisticated than that, even if you pretend not to be. I know you are. I read your English paper. We just want to know what you know."

"I'm not telling you anything about Jenny's dad."

Kracik cleared his throat. "Give me a second, Ted. Jaiden, Tate wants to make a lot of trouble for us. He's a fanatic and he's wrong. You know that plant's won awards; you know how proud we are of that. But if he starts convincing people his lies are true, that could cost us a lot of money. Good people could lose their jobs. Even Nancy."

Even Ben. Now I knew what had happened to him. He'd overheard them talking about grilling me for information and he told them exactly what he thought of it.

Ben got fired because of me.

I shook my head. "I'm not telling you anything."

Bungrin tried to sound friendly, but you could see behind his eyes how he was getting annoyed at all the time this was taking. "Kiddo, we know how you feel, but we wouldn't ask if it wasn't important."

"I don't have to tell you anything," I said, right to his smooth, smiling face. I turned to Nancy. "Nancy, tell them I don't have to tell them. It's my life."

Nancy lowered her head and Kracik got back into the act.

"Tate's planning to lie about us. We all know lying is wrong."

Except, according to the 4Bs, when it's to make you look better. If memory served, Carl Kracik had an autographed copy.

"We just want you to get this man talking a little, so we know what new lies he's planning to tell, so we can protect ourselves from his lies."

"No. No way. Conversation over. What are you going to do? Fire me?"

Bungrin looked at his watch, a fat Rolex that probably cost six billion dollars. "Let's spell it out. Jaiden, how do you feel about no more school?"

Not good, really, but I played my only card. "I'll tell the press. I'll tell them you asked me to spy on Mr. Tate."

Everyone leaned forward again, except Bungrin. The smile vanished from his face, like a light when you flip the switch. He spoke slowly, unhappy to take the time. "Go ahead. No one asked you to spy. Lie about it and we'll go public with your little crime spree. Any news about you would be white noise anyway if Tate's story gets out."

I was thinking I'd call his bluff, have him kick me out of school, the whole nine yards, rather than cave. Only one thing held me back.

"You gonna fire Nancy the same way you fired Ben?"

"Who's Ben?" Bungrin said. The Robo-Suit behind him whispered in his ear.

"The big-mouthed cook?"

Robo-Suit nodded.

"Jaiden, If I were you, I'd worry about me. How does a teen rehab camp sound? You know, with the drill sergeants, the drug addicts, and the accidental deaths?"

It was old Jeremy Banks's turn to clear his throat. "But if you play ball and we can make things easier for you. I don't know . . . send you and Jenny to Disney World for a week. Have breakfast with Mickey, on me."

I stood up. "I have to go to school."

Bungrin exhaled from his nose. "Okay. The newspaper interview gives us a lot to talk about anyway. But we'll meet again. Maybe just you and me, kiddo."

I was about to tell him exactly what I thought of his "kiddo" remark when he motioned toward Nancy. "Walk him to his ride. Try to convince him we're not the International League of Super Villains."

Yeah, that'd be real easy right after "Doc Doom" Bungrin had just done such a great job convincing me otherwise.

A few titters raced around the table at Ted's grand jest, but Nancy just nodded and stood. We walked out of the room together, me squeaking, she slumping.

She didn't say a word until we were in the elevator.

"This is serious, Jaiden. NECorp has a lot of money and prestige wrapped up in that plant. Eric Tate wants to make us the next Enron."

"And that makes it right to ask me to spy on my girl-friend's father?"

She looked at me. "I thought you said she wasn't your girlfriend."

"Forget I said that and answer the question."

She sighed. "You need to think about what Bungrin said. He'll do what he threatens, so you need to think about it carefully."

"But you don't think it's right, do you?"

The elevator doors swished. She stuck her laptop in to keep them from closing and came nearer so she could whisper. "You need to think about what Mr. Bungrin said. I could get fired for telling you anything else. Do you understand?"

I nodded. "Ben said I should tell NECorp to screw itself."

Nancy grimaced. "Ben's a good guy."

We came to the lobby. Tony's car was parked outside.

"I've got a lot to do, Jaiden. Have a good day at school," Nancy said, then she walked off. As she did, a sheet of paper slipped from her laptop case. It flitted in the air then slid onto the floor.

"Hey, Nancy, you dropped something," I said.

I said it pretty loud, but she didn't seem to hear me, so I trotted up to grab the paper. As I did, it dawned on me that Nancy *never* dropped anything. When I bent over to pick it up, I saw what it was. It was a confidential memo outlining NECorp's potential liability for the mercury pollution from the LiteSpring plant, which, as it turned out, was really four times greater, not 75 percent less like they'd announced.

Eric Tate was right. Bungrin and everyone else had been lying.

She'd dropped it on purpose. Numb, I stuffed the sheet into one of my books and headed out. Tony didn't bother saying a word to me for the whole trip.

By the time I reached school, it was lunchtime, so I went to the cafeteria. The place was packed, the sound like a low, deep beehive.

Nate was in our usual spot, toward the center of the big room. When he saw me, he waved me over. I headed toward him. I smiled a little, but the smile on my face made me think of Bungrin, so I stopped.

"Jai-den!" Nate said.

"I've got to tell you something," I said.

"What?"

"Hang on. You'll see."

But I didn't just tell him. Instead, I grabbed the top of one of those plastic trash bins and stood up on the table.

"Jaiden, what?"

Don't know why I did it, really. At first I was going to just tell Nate, but then I was like out of my body, watching myself. I slammed my hand against the trash-bin lid louder and louder. Pretty soon I had about a quarter of the cafeteria looking at me.

When I thought I had enough of them, I shouted, really loud: "My name is Jaiden Beale. I am the first person ever to be adopted and raised by a corporation."

"Who gives a crap?" someone screamed. "Sit down!"

"Google me! Google me now!" I screamed.

"Google yourself, retard!"

But someone else shouted, "Wait a minute, my dad told me about that story."

A buzz floated through the cafeteria, getting louder and louder.

"Whoa," Nate said, typing into his PDA.

I don't know if that was good or bad.

I was too busy thinking what Ben had told me. Screw NECorp.

II

DOTTING Ts, CROSSING EYES

I felt like I was astrally projecting when I did it, but it'd been what they call a calculated move. No way Bungrin could get me to spy for him. Eric Tate would know who I was. As for his threats, well, I hoped he wouldn't follow through because it wasn't worth it. It was like this Clint Eastwood movie where he and the bad guy both have guns, so the bad guy grabs Clint's daughter and holds his gun to her head.

"Move and I'll shoot her," he says.

Clint says, "Go ahead."

The guy gets all flustered. "You'd kill your own daughter?"

Clint says, "No. You will. Then I'll kill you. So why don't you just let her go?"

The bad guy, seeing the reason in this, lets her go.

Clint shoots him anyway, but hey, the point is if I was useless to Bungrin now, why punish me? It was part of my new screw NECorp campaign, dedicated to Ben.

Along those lines, I had one more thing to do, give Jenny the memo so she could give it to her dad. That'd get him the attention he needed, and force NECorp to clean up their act. Then, as Mr. Tate was given a Nobel prize for saving the earth, I'd swing down, grab Jenny, and take her out on my supercycle for fries and a shake. If not, at least Jenny might be proud of what I'd done and write to me at teen rehab.

Meanwhile, it turns out that having people gawk at you like you're a UFO flying down the hall is one of those feelings you just can't anticipate. It was kind of neat when it was a bunch of cute girls, but even the janitors gaped.

And search the halls as I might, I couldn't find Jenny.

Did see Nate, though, on my way to seventh period, and learned what he thought of the real me. He was grinning like a clown and talking like he'd swallowed a six-pack of cola.

"Come here you big lug," he said. "I'm gonna hug you whether you like it or not!"

He moved toward me like he was really going to do it, so I backed up. Not so big on the hugging. "Whoa, whoa, whoa!" I said. "You're not angry?"

"Sure, if you want. You could've told me, right? But hell, you just turned my life into a little piece of heaven!"

"And we are talking about what, exactly?

"Beeswax29! Caitlin! I know you, she knows I know you, so she's talking with her friends, yak-yak-yak Jaiden

Beale, can it be true? Yak-yak-yak, she sees me and walks up to talk to me! It's better than knowing a rock star! I even asked her out."

"You, Nate Buckman, asked Caitlin Fermelli out?"

"Actually, I asked if she needed help getting an adapter for her cell phone."

"What'd she say?"

"She said no. But then she checked out my PDA and now it's a maybe . . . if I loan her my cell phone. Her parents track her calls on hers. Isn't that medieval?"

"Dude," I said. "She's using you."

"I know! Isn't it great?"

He looked like he was going to try to hug me again, but instead he slammed his hand into my arm really hard, right in the old bandage, which I'd almost forgotten about.

"Ow!" I screeched.

"Isn't that better yet?" he asked, but before I answered he was trotting backward down the hall. "Gotta go. Caitlin's in next period! Call me tonight, you magnificent bastard!"

I rubbed my arm. It was throbbing. How long had it been since I cut it on the fence? Shouldn't it feel better by now instead of worse? I thought about the water I fell into, looking all oily and silver in the moonlight. Then I thought I really should get that memo to Jenny. But I never saw her.

When school finished, I stood out front, waiting. Finally, I spotted her, her hands buried in her pockets, her hair tied back as she walked resolutely through the crowd.

"Jenny! Jenny!" I called, but she kept walking.

I leaped right in front of her and said, "Hey!"

When she looked at me, I babbled about everything, about Ben, about the meeting, about how I'd finally done the exact opposite of what they expected of me, but all along she just kept shaking her head, like I was a channel she wanted to change.

"It's all over the net. My dad called and he was really furious. I'm not supposed to talk to you anymore. I told you I wasn't cool. I'm sorry."

I was stunned. Hadn't she heard me about the pollution and the memo? Or had I mentioned the memo? What had I said, exactly? I couldn't remember. I was about to shove the paper at her when it was suddenly snatched from my hands.

"Sorry, Jai," Tony said. "Nancy told me to grab any white papers you had."

"Wait! That proves . . ."

But Jenny had already taken off. And before I could finish, Eyeballs, who I'd thought of as a real man's man, stuck his fingers in his ears and said, "Nanananananananan! I can't hear you! Loo-loo-loo!"

Then he tore up the memo.

"Don't you even care what it says?" I screamed.

"No. Now, get in the car please."

Screw NECorp. Yeah, right. Screw Jaiden was more like it.

With Jenny and the memo gone, I was flummoxed,

which was a vocabulary word about a month ago. I stumbled back into the car. As we drove, Tony called Nancy and she met us at the front entrance, steaming.

The first thing she did when she saw me was grab me by the arm, pinching my wound under my coat.

"Isn't that feeling better yet?" she asked.

I shook my head, hoping for sympathy. Instead, she shoved me all the way to my suite where she slammed the door and started hissing and whisper-screaming. For someone who usually didn't show emotion, she shared beautifully.

"I gave you that memo so *you'd* know what was going on! Not so you could take it to your girlfriend!"

"She's not my girlfriend, she's not even talking to me! What'd you think I was going to do with it? If it's true, it's got to stop, right? People could get sick, right?"

"Of course, but we have to be careful about how we do it. LiteSpring is how Ted Bungrin made his name. Now the Veeps look at him like he's the CEO. If all this comes out, he's done for, but he could take down the whole company with him. All of NECorp."

"So, you're afraid of getting fired?"

"It's on the list, yes! Unless this is handled right thousands could lose their jobs. You lose, too. A bankrupt NECorp can't pay you when you come of age."

"I don't care about the money."

She glared. "Of course not. Why would you? You were

raised by a corporation, after all. Okay, let's try it the reasonable way."

She buttoned her suit jacket and tried to calm her voice. "Once you gave that memo to Eric Tate, it would prove there's someone inside NECorp leaking information. After that, anyone who didn't circle the wagons with Bungrin would be gone, and, in the end, so would the company. Is that what you want?"

I slumped in my chair. "You might have mentioned all this stuff beforehand."

"I wanted you to *read* it! You made such a big deal out of going to school, I couldn't tell you before because I was afraid people were listening. Who expected a quiet kid like you to start making major lunchroom announcements?"

I shrugged. "So what's the plan?"

She sat down herself and exhaled. "The truth will come out sooner or later, but if NECorp moves first it can control the situation. We have to shut down the plant, switch back to the old production method, apologize, and pay for the remediation. If we do that fast, the story might only last two or three news cycles and the damage would be minimal. But Bungrin will never do that. It'd be suicide for him. And, unfortunately, right now, there's only one person who can pull rank on him."

Even I knew who that was. "Hammond? You're going to talk to Mr. Wacky?"

She sighed. "He is the CEO, Jaiden, and he's not

always . . . wacky. And no, I'm not going to talk to him. I couldn't even get an appointment. *You're* going to talk to him. Yes, you. He likes you."

That much was true. Mr. Hammond always did like me, and I had a standing offer to visit whenever I wanted.

"I'll walk you up now."

"Now?"

"The longer we wait, the more chance Bungrin will find out what we're doing."

We took the main elevator to the fifth floor, which was, in its entirety, Mr. Hammond's office. The doors slid open and it was like the tomb of the Emperor Chin. China was named after this guy, so it doesn't get bigger. That place had over six thousand statues of soldiers, each different, and a model of the capital city, with (ironically) mercury in the rivers, to make it look like water. One of the seven gaudiest wonders of the world.

Mr. Hammond's outer office was kind of like that.

I'm serious. Rare birds flew in the air, and along one side ran a fake stream that fed a pond with goldfish. The stream ran the length of the room, then through the wall and into Mr. Hammond's office, right by his assistant's desk.

It was like visiting the Wizard of Oz.

Cheryl Diego, his assistant, was kind of short, but had an extremely pointy face. She always wore thick black glasses that looked like weapons. When she walked through the building, everyone cleared a path. When she saw me, though, she smiled and said, "Go right in, Jaiden. He'll be happy to see you."

With the stream beside me, I looked back at Nancy, hoping she might come with me, but we both knew that wasn't possible. It might look like she'd put me up to it and, if Bungrin found out, she'd be toast. So she gave me a little thumbs-up, the most blatant encouragement I think I've ever gotten from her, and hightailed it for the elevator.

Even the new doors to Hammond's office were weird. They were these huge black things he'd recently installed. They looked like monoliths. Expecting them to be heavy, I gave one a shove, shocked to see it swing in really fast. Fortunately, it had some kind of pneumatic braking system and didn't slam into the wall. It just sort of slowed by itself.

Inside was a landing strip for small aircraft that passed for a desk. The only thing on it was a blank yellow legal pad and a sharp pencil. But that wasn't what dominated the place. It was the water wall.

The stream in the waiting room was fed by a fountain twenty feet wide. Water came out of the ceiling in a steady solid gush that cascaded down a flat face of gray stone. If you looked carefully, you could see the NECorp logo etched in the stone. It was like NECorp had improved on nature.

Mr. Hammond stood in front of it, like he was standing in a rain forest. He wore a dark, comfortable suit that matched the stone. His curly hair was more salt than pepper, and he liked to let it grow into a wild, mangy mess so he reminded himself of Einstein.

As I came in, his face lit up with a warm grin, but his eyes, as always, sparkled with major insanity.

"Jaiden," he said, "if a tree falls in a forest and no one's there to hear it, does it make a sound?"

You have to know Mr. Hammond to appreciate the question. He used to show me a nickel and a dime when I was a kid and ask which I wanted. It's an old joke, but, okay, parts of my life are like bad movies and parts are like old jokes. Anyway, he always laughed when I took the nickel. This went on for years until he asked why I kept taking the larger nickel, even though the smaller dime was worth more.

I didn't really want the damn nickel or the damn dime anymore. (I figured I'd only made about $1.20 all together.) So I told him, "If I took the dime, you'd stop offering me money. So, really, I made more by taking the nickel."

I thought he'd be pissed, but he laughed his ass off and gave me twenty bucks. Back then it was nickels and dimes. These days it's philosophical questions, but silly ones, like the tree in the forest thing, or can God make a rock so big he can't lift it. I think it was his way of saying everything is silly, so it really didn't matter what you did.

But I liked to answer him anyway, in case there was another twenty coming.

"Sure it does," I said. "It has to."

"Ah," he said, raising a finger. "How do you know?"

I shrugged. "Same way you know there's a tree if there's no one there to see it."

He thought about it a second, then laughed, but I didn't get any money.

"It's a delight to watch your mind grow," he said. "I've watched this company grow, too, but it's not the same. Business I understand, but people are strange things."

He turned back to the water like it was a window. Sometimes I thought it was sad, but sometimes he seemed so tickled to hear himself talk I had to wonder if maybe he was really happy.

"People aren't built for modern life, Jaiden. Men aren't bred for suits and cars and cubicles, they were made to wander the antelope-filled plains, to hunt. It was simple in the past, whoever was strongest and fastest would be leader. If you got out of line, well, then the leader would just beat the crap out of you. Can you imagine?"

I was going to say, yeah, I thought I saw a movie or read about a war like that once, but he wasn't really asking. It was one of those rhetorical questions.

He raised an eyebrow. "It's still like that, but thanks to money, what constitutes strength is different. The weak can now hire muscle to do the crap beating. Maybe it's fairer, but someone still has to threaten to beat up someone else to make it work—or there'd be anarchy, barbarism.

148

"Did you know there was a major corporation in Japan that let their employees use bamboo sticks to beat dummies made to look like their foremen? Can't you see them Jaiden, whacking and screaming, maybe knocking the stuffing out of the dummy, maybe striking the head so hard that the bamboo splinters or their 'foreman's' face cracks? Wouldn't you like to do that to some teacher at your school?"

This time he really was asking, so I said, "I don't hate any of them that much."

He nodded. "You're a kind young man. That's how we raised you. And of course, we don't allow that here at NECorp, but we do have a gym, and who knows what people think when they're playing basketball or running on the treadmill? I used to pretend I was being chased by a tiger. Then I started pretending I was the tiger. Much more satisfying."

He smiled to himself. "What do you like to pretend to be, Jaiden?"

"I like Star Wars," I offered. Not that I run around pretending I'm Darth Vader anymore, but I didn't feel like explaining Gandhi and the Hulk to him.

"Good," he said with a little smile. "Good."

That's what Mr. Hammond was like, jumping from Japan to treadmills to tigers. Some people thought that made him brilliant, but really, doesn't he just sound nuts?

Before he went off on another tangent, I thought I'd get to the point: "Mr. Hammond, I know about the pollution from LiteSpring, how it's worse than ever."

He sighed. The sound of it mixed with the rush of clean water. Then he looked off, like a cat focusing on something invisible in midair.

"Oh, that," he said. Then he actually stepped away from the wall, walked toward his huge desk, and leaned on it. "A serious business. Frankly, I wish you didn't know about it, but you're old enough to understand that sometimes when you try to do good, you wind up doing harm instead. Then the question becomes, how do you get out of it doing the least additional damage?"

I shrugged. "Isn't honesty the best policy?"

He shook his head. "Oh, no, Jaiden. Maybe in love, but . . . scratch that, not even in love. The problem with truth is that people have different truths. Take my little waterfall. I look at it and see the essence of life, shapeless, yet informing everything, filling my heart, my lungs, my mind, my soul, making the world alive with meaning. Someone else might see a waste of water, resources that might better be used to feed a starving village."

"So . . . why don't you feed the village?"

He smiled. "Yes, yes, why don't we just feed the world? Give the people what they need? After all, NECorp is rich! The problem with giving away everything is that then you have nothing left to give, then even more people go hungry and you go hungry yourself. But . . . if you build businesses and businesses create jobs, the giving can go on forever, until it's Christmas every day!

"At the level I work, Jaiden, everything is very, very abstract, but very, very important. If I make one decision over another, it could cost or create thousands of jobs, millions of dollars could be made or evaporate into the air. Just evaporate. I need a clear mind and the freedom to let it explore. My water wall helps me, and that helps everyone. If it helped me make just one million-dollar decision, don't you think it's worth it?"

"I don't know—how much does it cost?"

And couldn't you get yourself, like, a dog instead?

He spun abruptly. "That's not the point. Do you think NECorp is evil? Do you think we want to be pouring mercury into the rivers here like it was soda pop?"

Geez, like soda pop?

"No sir, I don't."

He put his hands on my shoulders. "Of course not. We've made you smarter than that. I must do something about it, but it has to be the right move. NECorp isn't just a building, Jaiden. What about our investors? Some people think all our stockholders are wealthy, but a lot are retired, living on fixed incomes. I've met some, during a . . . holiday, I think. We can't just abandon them because we made a mistake, can we?"

"No, sir."

He stepped back. "Good."

He looked at his water wall again. "Since you know about it, here's another question for your young mind. I don't expect you to have the correct answer, because maybe there isn't one, but what do *you* think is the right thing to do about LiteSpring?"

He meant it as an exercise, to show how tough it was to face the kind of problems he dealt with every day, but really, he just lobbed it right over the plate at me, didn't he?

I pretty much repeated what Nancy said: "The truth is going to come out sooner or later, so I'd move first in order to control the situation. Shut down the plant, go back to old production methods, apologize, and pay for the remediation. Move quick and it might only last two or three news cycles. Any damage could be minimal."

He kind of stumbled backward so the back of his head got splashed with water from the fountain. He shook his head to get the water off, then came forward, narrowing his eyes, looking a little like that tiger he liked to pretend to be. I thought he was going to scream and accuse me of being someone's mouthpiece, but as big drops of water hit the shoulders of his expensive suit and ran down the front, he laughed.

"That's it!" he said. "Perfect! We have to be proactive! It's simple. It's strong."

He was so happy, I felt like asking him if I could have a big fountain, too.

"I'll move on this at once."

He walked over to his desk, grabbed that single yellow legal pad and pencil, and started scribbling.

I was thinking, hey, mission accomplished, time to get the hell out of there. But just as I was about to make myself scarce, the monolith doors swung open and in stepped none other than our Senior Vice President of Evil, Teddy Bear Bungrin.

When he saw me, a huge grin swelled on his face, like it was infected.

"Jaiden! There you are, kiddo!"

He actually reached forward and mussed my hair.

Mr. Hammond looked up. I was expecting him to fire the creep then and there, but he just smiled. "Ted, I see you've made the acquaintance of our young ward."

"Sure have," Ted answered. "In fact, I was just searching the whole damn building for the scamp. And of course he was in the last place I looked. Ha."

"Glad you're here. We need to have a chat about LiteSpring. I've made some decisions," Mr. Hammond said. Then he gave me a wink.

Bungrin didn't blink. "Sure, Desmond."

Mr. Hammond nodded at me. "Why don't you get going, Jaiden? Ted and I may have to wrassle a bit!" He moved his hands and shoulders like he was with the WWE.

Ted smiled, I smiled, Mr. Hammond smiled. We were all smiling, but none of us meant it. Maybe it was all the ozone in the air, but I started to feel that suit growing on me again.

Brrr.

As I headed out, Bungrin grabbed me by the arm—the one with the bandage. It hurt like hell, but I wasn't going to let him know that.

"Oh, kiddo, heard about your speech in school today. In fact, it's all over the papers. Good move. You're off the hook with me and now you'll be famous with your friends. Stupid idea on my part, I guess. Now go do your homework."

His tone was chilling, but even that didn't dampen my mood. Mr. Hammond was going to make NECorp do the right thing. Maybe in a couple of days, I could tell Jenny about it, and maybe her dad would change her mind about me and the company and . . .

I raced off to tell Nancy the news.

12

MERGERS AND INQUISITIONS

Think they'll whack this Ted Bungrin guy?"

I stared at Nate's jagged little picture on my laptop and made a face.

"No. Geez, this is a corporation, not the Mafia."

I never would've gotten the webcam to work if Nate hadn't walked me through it. There was some Flash memory I had to upgrade, and the guys in our Information Technology (IT) department get totally wonky if they have to do anything aside from install or uninstall MS Office.

"But you'd *like* them to whack him, wouldn't you?"

"Sure. It'd probably improve the gene pool."

"So what do you think is going to happen for real?"

I was sitting on my bed. Nancy had been thrilled with the news about my meeting with Hammond and there wasn't much homework, so it turned out to be a quiet night for a change. And I did owe Nate a call.

"They'll hang him out to dry in front of the press, then

buy out his contract, giving him millions of dollars just to pack his desk," I said. "And Jenny's dad will give me some sort of award for environmental excellence."

I laid back and imagined Jenny kissing me at the ceremony. I shifted a little onto my arm and a throbbing pain from the cut washed the daydream out of my head.

Nate poked his head around the screen, looking confused. "Where'd you go? I'm staring at a wall with some loser Star Wars poster on it."

"Sorry." I held the laptop up over me so the little camera pointed at my face. The thing was about the size of a dime. "How's that?"

"Better. Except now I *do* see your face."

I blew a half-raspberry at him. "Get used to it. I'm all over the damn place."

"I know. You getting calls from the papers and the cable channels?"

"No. My line's pretty private. So don't you go giving away the number, Nate, okay? It could really screw me."

"Hey, me you can trust. I owe you my very existence, remember?"

I leaned over to look out the window, but twisted the laptop so Nate could still see me. "There are news vans out front, you know, with those huge satellite feed antennas? But security keeps kicking them off the property. Nancy's fielding all the interview requests. She says we may have to have a press conference tomorrow afternoon, just to keep them from camping out. I may get to go on *Oprah*."

"*Oprah?* Please. Hold out for *The Daily Show* or *South Park*."

"I don't think I can guest star on an animated show, Nate."

"Sure you can. They do it all the time. You can just do the voice-over."

"Actually that sounds pretty cool. Ha! I can do a confession about how my corporate parent beats me."

"Yeah, well, watch out in school tomorrow. I've got a feeling Deever isn't as secure as NECorp."

Huh. He had a point. And not just on top of his head.

"Hey! Gotta go! Caitlin's IMing me!"

I raised an eyebrow. "She still got you wrapped around her little finger?"

"No! I said *she* was IMing *me*, right? Okay, so maybe I gave her the PDA as a permanent loan sort of thing. But I've still got my laptop. Sure, maybe it's a little older, but . . ."

I shook my head at him. "You are such a sucker."

Nate shrugged and the screen went blank. As it turned out, I never had anything to worry about with Nate. He thought my situation was cool. Didn't even blink, really. Felt lucky to know me. At the time, I was feeling pretty lucky to know me myself.

After not sleeping last night, I slept like a log and woke up a little late. It wasn't until I went to breakfast that I remembered Ben was gone. I made a mental note to write to him as soon as I got back from school. I didn't even order home fries. I had the French toast, and some sausages. It just didn't seem right to order eggs and bacon from someone else. Not yet, anyway. It was too soon.

Eyeballs drove me to school, but I didn't feel much like talking to him, which made for a very quiet trip. After he realized I was still pissed at him for grabbing the memo, he just turned the car radio up loud and we bobbed our heads to some trashy alternative rock.

I suppose I shouldn't have been angry with him. He was just following Nancy's orders, and, really, that had turned out for the best, hadn't it? Now NECorp had a chance to do the right thing itself, and even if everyone did know my secret, at least I wouldn't have to be totally ashamed.

What came next made me feel a little better about ol' Eyeballs. There were a bunch of reporters out in front of the school, with video cameras, interviewing kids on their way to class. It wasn't until I got out of the car and all the interviews suddenly stopped and the reporters came rushing in my direction, that I realized they'd been asking those kids about me.

"Is NECorp sending you to public school because they're too cheap to send you to a good school?"

"Do they let you date?"

"Do they give you a curfew?"

"Do you have a Web site?"

"Is it true NECorp is raising you without any religion?"

"What do you think of Eric Tate's accusations against LiteSpring?"

It wasn't like I could have answered even if I'd wanted to. They were like a bunch of human-sized bugs, swarming, shoving mikes in my face. And here's where Tony showed his stuff. He got himself between me and the paparazzi, wedged his way through, and pulled me along, all the while saying loudly, "The press conference is at NECorp tonight. No questions until then. Give the kid a break, he's got to get to school."

Not that they listened, but he was big enough to be intimidating and moving fast enough to make a difference, so we made it all the way to the front door. There, Deever's security guards, whom I'd always thought of as sort of lazy given all the contraband that gets through, took over, and stopped anyone who wasn't a student from coming inside.

I popped into the school hallway like a bubble from the bottom of a glass of soda. Then, of course, as I walked along, there were the stares again, but people were getting a little bolder and I suddenly found out I had all these friends I'd never met before.

"You need something, you ask me," some truck-sized guy said in homeroom. I'd never seen him speak before, so I'd always figured he was mute. More than one girl gave me a big smile, too. Nate asked me to sign an autograph for Caitlin, which was totally weird, and Ms. Chrob actually seemed nervous when she was talking to me, stumbling over her words and stuff.

But Jenny, Jenny barely looked at me.

I had to actually corner her after class.

"Will you talk to me? Just for a minute?" I said, trotting up alongside her.

She stopped. She shook her head. "I'm not supposed to."

"Come on! I'm not the enemy here! I've got some stuff I have to tell you. Good stuff. Really good stuff. Stuff so good you won't even believe it's real stuff."

She stopped and looked at me. "Like what kind of stuff?"

I looked around. Six other kids had stopped, too. They were pretending to look away, like they weren't paying attention, but it was so obvious.

"I can't tell you here."

"Then forget it," she said, and she started walking again.

"No, no, no, no!" I cut her off again and leaned in close.

She pulled back, maybe thinking I was going to kiss her, but I just gritted my teeth and whispered in her ear.

"Give me a second. After school, Tony's going to park in front and they're going to send me out the back, so the press won't corner me. Just meet me there and walk me across the field. Just across the field. Five minutes I promise, you'll want to hear it. Your dad will want to hear it."

She looked up and made a face. She looked down and made another face.

"Come on," I begged.

"Okay," she finally said. "Now can I please get to class?"

I stepped aside and swept my arm out for her. I thought this was kind of cute and endearing, until some of the kids following me around did exactly the same and all of a sudden she was running this gauntlet of swept arms.

"Will you give me a break?" I said to them.

The rest of the school day was unusual, to say the least. Shanna Denton had apparently forgotten about the ugly Hello Kitty incident and started trying to flirt with me. Mr. Abbate implied he'd raise my Spanish grade if I appeared in a commercial for his brother's used car dealership. There were more incidents like that. Mostly they involved offers and requests from fellow students and their parents, like asking me to appear at fund-raisers.

Anyway, the last bell finally rang. Security escorted me to a small room while the halls cleared, then to the rear exit. There's a concrete pavilion just before the football field, and you could see for miles around that no one was there, except for the limo waiting for me at the far end of the field.

As the security guard opened the door for me, he spotted Jenny sitting on a bench, wrapping her arms around herself for warmth. He looked like he was about to chase her off, but I shook my head. "It's okay. She's my friend. She's walking me." He nodded and closed the door.

I walked up, Jenny stood, and we started across the

field. Not a word for the first few yards. I didn't know where to begin exactly, but I knew I was glad to be with her and afraid that if I didn't say just the right thing, she wouldn't stay very long.

But what did I have to worry about, really? I did good, didn't I? I talked the CEO into coming clean about the pollution, after all. But what if that wasn't enough for her and her dad? Mr. Tate looked like he was out for blood. He might have preferred it if NECorp went belly-up.

Jenny was wearing denim overalls. The straps were hidden under her coat, but the pants ended mid-calf and she had on ankle socks that made for a lot of bare leg. Anyway, I was looking down as we walked, and I guess I was staring at her legs, because she turned and looked at me with an annoyed expression on her face, like I was staring at her like she was a piece of meat.

"Yeah?" she said.

"Aren't you freezing in those?" I asked, trying to pretend that was really what I was thinking.

She shook her head, "no," but then smiled a little and said, "Yes. I am. So why don't you tell me what you wanted to say so I can go inside somewhere?"

Since now it meant I was keeping her out in the cold, I started.

"But you have to promise not to tell anyone."

"Jaiden."

"Especially your dad."

"Jaiden."

"Really. A lot of people could get in a lot of trouble if what I'm about to tell you gets out early, so you have to promise not to tell."

"Okay. Fine. I promise."

With that, I launched into an explanation of what happened yesterday between me and Mr. Hammond, hoping that Jenny would be pleased. Instead, she furrowed her brow for the longest time. We were walking all the while, and the limo was getting closer and closer, so I was starting to be afraid that our walk would end with her brow still furrowed and without her saying a word.

But finally she stopped. "That's good, Jaiden, I guess, but even if the plant goes back to the old levels, the mercury is still dangerous. Do you know it's been pumping that stuff into the water and the air for almost twenty years? I mean, really, the plant should be shut down permanently, or moved somewhere further away from drinking water."

"But . . . I mean . . . is there really enough mercury in the water to make anyone actually sick?"

"My dad's trying to figure that out, but so far the only thing he's come up with is a small rise in local autism rates."

"Autism? You mean like when people can't read emotions?"

"Yeah. Mercury can affect fetuses, and there are some

studies that link it directly to autism, but they're controversial. The rise in autism here goes back to when the plant was first built. It's not something you can just fix. And you're part of it."

"Guess there aren't any fluorescent bulbs in your house, huh?"

"No, there aren't."

She had me there. "So what do you think I should do?"

She looked at me. Her nose was red from the cold and she rubbed it a little with her hand. "Tell my dad what you told me. Tell the press. Don't let NECorp just clean it up. Make them close it down."

"I can't. The scandal could bring down the whole corporation. Everyone could be fired. A lot of lives could be ruined."

"So? NECorp's not your parent, Jaiden. It's a company, a company that's poisoning people."

"It's not just a thing. It's the people in it. I mean, a lot of the investors live on a fixed income and . . ."

She shook her hands in frustration. "Aghh! Do you believe what you're saying? Do you even know if it's true? Jaiden, I like you. I think you're a good guy, but isn't it about time you became your own person?"

I stood there thinking about everything she said, my head spinning in all sorts of directions at once. Everything I thought I should do seemed wrong somehow, like there was no right answer. The whole poisoning thing was sticking out loud and clear, but then all of a sudden, her last sentence struck me, and I clung to it like it was the only thing floating in the big black sea I was drowning in.

"You're a funny one to talk about being your own person," I told her.

Her face scrunched up. "What do you mean?"

"Well, look at you, you say you like me, but you're doing exactly what your dad is telling you and not hanging out with me anymore. Is that what someone who's their own person would do? You're always worried about being 'cool'—is that cool?"

She kept her face scrunched up for a while. A bit of wind whipped through her hair. I could see the tiny wool fibers on the strands of her knitted cap twitch and shiver in the air as she thought.

"You're right."

I was?

"Of course I'm right," I said.

She looked nervous, but kind of happy about it. "So, do you want to work on our project some more this afternoon?"

"You mean now?"

"Yes. Now. My dad's at a big meeting at his office."

I shrugged. "Sure. Do you want to head to your house?"

"No. I'm not sure exactly when he'll be back. How about yours?"

"Uh . . . I don't have a house, remember?"

"Sure you do. A great big one. You live at NECorp, right?"

"Yeah."

"So take me there. I'd really like to see it."

I thought about it. No way would Nancy let the daughter of Eric Tate into the building, not with the press outside and all the hush-hush negotiations going on. Jenny just wouldn't be trusted. But heck, *I* trusted her. And what could she see anyway if we just went to my room? I'd already told her all the important stuff.

But how to get her inside?

"Okay, but you're going to have to trust me about something else, too."

She furrowed her brow. "What?"

About half an hour later, I met her on her bike at one of the loading docks outside NECorp. Deliveries arrived mostly in the morning, and with security focused on the press out front, the place was empty enough for me to sneak something relatively small inside, something like Jenny.

Not that she was wild about hiding in a garbage can. I brought out one of those big orange suckers with huge wheels and a nice tight lid, the cleanest I could find. After I showed it to her and assured her it was disinfected, she kind of got into the idea that it would be fun to sneak into NECorp.

She tossed her books in and tried to climb in after them. I had to steady the can a bit and help heft her, which was kind of cool. I think she smiled at me as I put my arm around her waist. Once she was in the can, I sealed her up nice and tight and wheeled her inside and into the service elevator.

The service elevator let us out in a corridor right near my suite, so I was able to wheel her in without anyone noticing. Unfortunately, it was right then that I noticed what a total wreck my room was. Comic books, video games, and laundry all over the place.

She started rapping on the lid and whispering, "Is it safe yet? Is it safe?"

I whispered back, even though no one could hear: "Uh, can you wait a minute?"

In a frenzied attempt at tidying, I kicked stuff under the desk and bed. Less than twenty seconds later, though, while I stood there with a bunch of dirty underpants in my hands, the lid of the trash can popped open and Jenny burst out.

She looked around, laughing. "It's . . . it's an office. All the furniture, the rugs, everything, it's totally corporate. How could this be your room?" Then she turned to me and noticed the pile of underwear I was holding. I dropped it immediately and grinned.

"Did you notice the plasma TV?" I asked, nodding toward it.

I flipped it on to one of the local news channels. Interestingly enough, they had a baby picture of me up on the screen, over the announcer's shoulder. I didn't change the channel, since it was a cute picture, but I did grin sheep-ishly.

Jenny shook her head. "It's your room, alright."

She put her hands on the rim of the can and realized she couldn't get out alone. "Help me out," she said.

"Love to." But no sooner did I walk over, then a rapping came at the door.

"Jaiden! Jaiden! Are you in there?"

I knew the voice. "Oh crap! It's my manager!"

"Your manager?"

"Yeah. Nancy. I can't let her see you. Get down."

For some reason, Jenny picked right then to try to be funny. "What? I'm not good enough to meet your man-ager?"

Ha-ha.

I stared at her while Nancy knocked again. "Not while your dad is trying to bring down the company! Now quit kidding around and get down!"

I pushed the lid back over her and opened the door. Nancy tried to step in, but I was in the way and didn't move.

"I just wanted to tell you there've been a ton of high-level meetings all day, put together by Mr. Hammond. I don't know the details, but they're planning an announce-ment soon. It looks like . . . it looks like things are swinging our way."

She was talking fast and had this expression on her

face that looked very unusual. It took a second for me to register what it was. A smile. Nancy was smiling.

She was happy.

After the big speech I'd just gotten from Jenny about mercury poisoning, I really didn't know how to feel about "things swinging our way," but I figured the least I owed Nancy was a "That's great!"—which I gave her.

"The announcement may bounce your press conference. If they fire Bungrin, it may push you out of the news cycle entirely. It's so . . . it's so . . . why is there a garbage can in the middle of your room?"

We both looked back at it, sitting there.

"I'm just . . . I'm just throwing out some old junk."

She smiled at me. "Well, you really are growing up a bit this week, aren't you?"

She didn't know the half of it.

You could see she was just bursting with all this feeling. For the first time since we met, she actually reached out and patted me on the shoulder. I smiled at her and tried to pretend it wasn't the most incredibly awkward thing ever.

"I'll let you know as soon as I do. I have to go back to listening at the door to the conference room now."

She waved and walked off. I shut the door and exhaled before pulling the lid off the can. Jenny was curled up in the bottom, looking up at me.

"I really should tell my dad," she said.

"No, you shouldn't." I answered. I reached in and pulled her to standing. We were pretty close, separated only by the orange plastic of the garbage can.

"Look, once this Bungrin guy is history, I'll work on getting Mr. Hammond to shut down the plant or move it."

"Come on. You can't even have a friend over to your room and tell your manager about it. You really think you can influence NECorp's decisions on something that big?"

I ran my finger along the lip of the plastic can, near her shirt. "The CEO loves me like a son."

"Oh, he does, does he?"

"Yeah, really."

I looked up at the same time she looked at me. Her green eyes were perfect and her pupils were opening up a bit. Her lips turned up, just a little, into this half smile like the one on that famous painting, *Mona Lisa.*

"You know, Jaiden, I think maybe you can."

I kind of moved forward a little, testing the air between us. It was such a little move forward it could have just been me shifting my balance on my feet. I knew, of course that it wasn't, but I had my story all ready in case she pushed me away.

But she didn't. She leaned forward, too. Shifting *her* balance.

Seemed ridiculous to stop, so we both kept going forward. This time the lawyers didn't break in and Jenny didn't freak and run away. This time our lips met. I drew her in, putting my hands on her upper back, pulling her closer as we kissed.

After that, things get a little fuzzy for me. There was more kissing, lots of it, and I remember our teeth clicking at one point, but mostly my entire brain was going, "Whoa!"

Until, out of nowhere, she pulled back and said, "Stop!"

"What?" I said, my eyes half-open. I thought I was dreaming.

"Jaiden, stop," she said again. But I was totally lost in the moment, so I kind of didn't and she, apparently not so lost in the moment, pulled away, angry.

"Jaiden, I said, stop!"

That was confusing. "What? Am I doing it wrong or something?"

"No, no! Look at the TV!"

She was so upset, I did. Where there used to be an old baby picture of me, there was now a picture of her dad, Eric Tate. The announcer was saying something about, "an unfriendly takeover by NECorp that's left JenCare company founder and consumer advocate Eric Tate apparently out in the cold."

Jenny pulled away from me and started climbing out of the can in this crazed effort to get closer to the TV, like that would make some kind of difference. She looked like she was going to fall over, so I tried to grab her and help her out, but she was squirming so much, we got all tangled. The garbage can tipped and she fell out.

She swatted at me as she got to her feet, landing a good one right on my bad arm, and then we both just stood there awhile, watching the news. Apparently, the big announcement from NECorp, the one that Nancy thought was going to be about things going "our way" was really that they had bought Mr. Tate's remediation company JenCare, and fired Mr. Tate.

As Jenny watched, her face got all pale. Then it got kind of puffy and her eyes got all watery. She twisted her head back and forth trying to hold it in, not wanting to weep in front of me I guess, but then tears started falling and she half-screamed, half-cried, "How could I ever have trusted you?"

And you know what happened next?

Jenny freaked and ran away.

13

TO B2B OR NOT TO B2B

I stood there staring at the screen as they repeated the story, unable to believe it. How the hell did Mr. Hammond, wacky though he may be, go from doing the exact right thing to the exact wrong thing in just twenty-four hours? Then it hit me.

In all the excitement, I forgot. Even Nancy forgot. Like I said earlier, Mr. Hammond was also famous for his tendency to agree with whoever he spoke with last.

And I'd left him alone in a room with Ted Bungrin.

I kicked the garbage can Jenny had been hiding in, kicked open my door, then stormed past Marketing & PR, knocking over a small trash can. I expected someone to say *something*, but the staff was hunched over their computer screens as if someone had drained their batteries. At the elevator I kept jamming the button like it would make the car show up faster.

As the little green circle lit up, Nancy came racing down the hall. "Jaiden, wait."

All the energy in her voice was gone. She sounded like a bored robot, which only made me madder. Shouldn't she be furious, too?

The elevator door didn't open fast enough, so I kicked that, too. The kick made a really satisfying crunking sound and left a nice big dent in the shiny silver surface. I was wedging myself into the sliver of an opening when she reached me.

"Something's happened," the Nancy-unit said.

I tumbled into the elevator and spun to face her. "I know! I know something's happened! I saw it on the news!"

She closed her eyes a second. "No, you don't understand."

I slammed the button for the top floor over and over. "Yes, yes I do. I'm not a kid! You work for a company that poisons people and me, I'm a decoration! Just like that stupid statue in the lobby. Expensive? Sure. But it impresses the investors."

Nancy shut her eyes again and this time didn't open them. I kicked the elevator wall. The door closed and I stood in a corner, feeling my blood boil, trying to figure out how I'd gone from my first kiss to the end of the world in less then ten minutes.

By the time I reached the top floor, my foot was throbbing. It's not such a great idea to go around kicking things really hard, especially metal things. When the doors slid open, they wobbled and squeaked. I was actually happy about that, maybe like Ranker had been when he stole the

Herbert statue. But then I felt bad for the poor guy who'd have to figure out how to fix it.

Trying to steady my breath so I didn't look like a psychotic ox, I walked past Cheryl Diego without even looking at her.

"I'm sorry, you can't . . . ," she said, but I ignored her. I know it was rude, but what was she talking about? Of course I could. I thought about kicking in the office doors, but my foot hurt too much, so I shoved them. They flew open, then did that pneumatic braking thing.

Mr. Hammond stood with his back to me, staring at the water wall like it was the whole universe. Sometimes I think the stupid bastard could forget the real world existed.

Well, I planned to remind him.

I was about to start yelling, when I noticed his hair was different. His height was off, too. His shoulders were too wide. Even his suit looked different. He turned around, and it wasn't Mr. Hammond at all.

It was Ted Bungrin, flashing his Satan smile at me. I looked around. The office was pretty much the same, but instead of Mr. Hammond's pad on the desk, there was Bungrin's laptop, looking like it owned the place.

I felt like I was going to throw up.

"Nice place, huh? I'll make some changes, but I think I'll keep the fountain."

"Where's Mr. Hammond?"

Bungrin's eyes got all sparkly. "Licking his wounds, I guess. He tried to take me down, and I won. Doctors heal the sick, carpenters build things, and people like me, win."

"It's not a game," I said. Then I got all flustered. "What . . . what'd you win?"

"Ha. We had a special meeting of the board of directors today, during which Mr. Hammond was voted out, and I was voted in. I'm the new CEO."

"No way."

Bungrin's smile widened. "Yes. It is, most definitely, way."

He reached out and put his finger in the water cascading down the wall. A big upside-down V appeared beneath his finger. You could see the rock wall under it, only instead of slick and cool, it looked cheap and plastic. This guy could make even water look wrong.

"I don't know what the old man expected me to do," he said.

"What *did* you do?"

He shrugged. "I told the board how much his 'remediation' plan would cost, and how little evidence there was that the mercury was doing real damage. That whole autism thing, the science is so anecdotal. You don't put a huge corporation in the red for a theory. When I told them I'd been in touch with one of the senior partners at Jen-Care who was more than happy to sell us his shares, they applauded."

He turned away from the wall and stepped toward me.

"I don't blame you, kiddo, for doing what you thought was right. If anything, I owe you. If you hadn't talked Hammond into this whole crazy honesty thing, I wouldn't have moved against him for at least three years. So, thanks."

He stuck his hand out. Water dripped from his finger to the floor, making a little gray circle on the rug. When I didn't move, he put it back down.

"I'm not a bad guy. Don't get me wrong, I'm not a good guy, either. But I am CEO. That makes me your new daddy, so don't you think we should learn to get along?"

"That plant is poisoning people."

"Anytime you put anything into the world, it gets dirty. You want beef for billions of burgers? You chop down rain forests to feed the cattle. You want fossil fuels? You get global warming. Cheap light for hospitals and libraries? You get mercury. I didn't get transferred here because I was saving the environment, I got transferred here because production went through the roof and the levels were still legal."

I stared at him. "I don't care if it's illegal or not, it's wrong."

"Blah, blah, blah. It's wrong. Blah, blah, blah. People get sick. Blah, blah, blah, the plant doesn't do what we said. Please. Blame the regulations that make it legal. So maybe we spend a lot trying to influence those regulations, but can you blame us? I'm just trying to make a profit. I'm sure we've even got some very dedicated people out there somewhere trying to figure out how to make things even better and greener for everyone. Maybe you can grow up and be the guy who can make light come out of people's butts for free. Meanwhile, life goes on, so can we at least agree to disagree?"

He stuck his hand out again.

I narrowed my eyes. "Why do you care what I think?"

He put the hand back down again. "You'll figure it out yourself in about twenty minutes, but I have a meeting in ten, so . . . Your speech at school put you back in the limelight. It'd be easier for both of us if we were on the same page, say, for a couple of news cycles. I wouldn't ask you to say anything you didn't want to, just not to comment on things a fourteen-year-old isn't really qualified to venture an opinion on anyway. Is that such a big deal? There must be some new game console you want. It's yours. I'll slip you a few R-rated DVDs. I'll hire back that short-order cook. What's his name? Glen?"

"Ben. He'd never work for you again."

"Oh?"

He held up his cell phone and pressed a button on it. Ben's recorded voice filled the room.

"Okay, Mr. Bungrin. I'd like to come back next week."

"See, all Glen—excuse me—Ben ever had to do was apologize. At first he was about his ideals, but I guess his empty wallet caught up with him. Now, I don't *have* to welcome him back. So, console, DVDs, and Ben, all in exchange for no comment."

He waited, but I was just stunned. He looked at his watch, all silver and shiny like the water on the wall, then sighed and rolled his eyes. "Okay, let's get more realistic. Here's your alternative: Say what you want about whatever you want and we smear your butt as a self-centered, ungrateful, teenage delinquent who's unhappy and unbalanced because we didn't buy you a pony. NECorp admits defeat at being your guardian, a ridiculous idea from a former CEO, and, after the rehab camp with the marines, you get placed on some antidepressants in a foster home in Idaho. I'll even fire your manager Nancy just because I think she had a little something to do with all this."

I started grinding my teeth. Was this guy Satan, or what?

"I'm not offering to shake hands again. Now, do we want poor Ben to show up and find out he doesn't have a job waiting, or are *you* going to put *your* hand out? It's time, kiddo."

And do you know what I did? That's right.

I freaked and ran out of the room.

"Fine," Bungrin shouted after me. "I'll know you by your deeds."

I ran, limping, for the elevator, without the slightest idea what I was going to do. I only knew I wanted to get away, just for a while. After ditching my cell phone in a garbage can, in case they wanted to track me, I found my bike and a warm jacket and sneaked out via the loading docks. I walked my bike along the building's edge, then through the small adjacent patch of woods. Finally, I hit a side street and started pedaling.

My foot still hurt, and my arm was aching again, so I took it nice and slow, not really thinking, just feeling all sorts of variations of numb inside.

By nightfall, I wound up back at the shopping center where that cop almost caught me. Curious, I cruised past the windows of Herbert's Burgers and peeked inside. On the counter was a new statue of Herbert, eyes still different sizes, like a birth defect. Ranker was there, too. He was emptying small trash bins into a big one, staring at the ground. I guess business had gotten better and they hired him back. Nothing had changed. The great fast-food machine was up and running again.

I rode on, back to the alley, where the tear in the chain-link fence had yet to be repaired. I dropped my bike by the fence and climbed into the woods. The moon was out and my eyes adjusted quickly to the darkness, so it was easy enough for me to find my way to the edge of that concrete runoff I'd fallen into.

A cold wind blew, my arm ached like crazy. I sat against a concrete pylon, curling up for warmth. I listened to the water. It didn't sound like the water in the fountain in Mr. Hammond's, I mean, Bungrin's, office. It sounded thick, like syrup.

If what Bungrin said about legal mercury levels was true, even if I had the memo it wouldn't mean anything. So maybe the EPA would withdraw its Excellence Award. Big deal.

So what could I do, really? Embarrass Bungrin? What about Ben and Nancy? And no, I didn't want to die in teen rehab or go to Idaho and never see Nate or Jenny again.

I put my head back against the concrete, felt the rough surface against my skull, and shut my eyes. Just a few more years and I'd be rich for the rest of my life. I could hire Ben myself, hire Eric Tate and send him to Washington to change the mercury guidelines.

So why not cave just for now?

Because Bungrin was a total ass?

No, because it felt wrong.

I remembered all those people who sued cigarette companies for selling them the tobacco that gave them cancer. I knew what Bungrin would say. Could you blame those companies for not checking out the health issues too closely or hiring scientists to prove the whole cancer thing was a mistake? Can you really be surprised that they'd lie?

It's like building this really cool ultrarobot, full of guns and lasers, programming it to be a perfect killing machine, then being totally shocked when it shoots you and doesn't understand for the life of it why you think it's wrong.

Foot and arm hurting, I fell asleep. I wish I'd dreamed about Jenny, but I didn't. Or maybe I did, but I just didn't remember.

When I woke, it was morning, but there wasn't a single bird chirping. My arm was the part of my body that hurt least. All my muscles ached and my head throbbed. My nose was stuffy and I didn't have a tissue. I wiped my eyes, stood, and stretched.

I was about to find my bike and head home, maybe try to talk to Nancy, but as I stared at the water and rubbed my arm, something dawned on me and instead, I followed the concrete runoff upstream. It ended a quarter mile later, with an iron grate in a hillside. If you looked up the hillside, you could see a fence and a building, and the building had a big, beautiful sign on it, a logo really:

LiteSpring.

I flashed back to what Jenny said about mercury and autism, how the plant had been poisoning the water for twenty years. I thought about how Ranker couldn't look people in the eye. My arm twinged, and I wondered what kind of gunk had gotten into it.

Okay, so maybe Ranker was a coincidence, but I knew how my arm felt. Standing there, it was hard *not* to see it, the plant in the background, the runoff all sparkly and shining, more like the river in the model Emperor Chin had in his tomb.

Everything just looked and smelled wrong.

And that was, at least to me, the truth.

It was getting late, and I was still thinking I'd be going to school that day, so I biked back. It was warmer than the night had been and the sun dried my sinuses.

I planned to sneak in through the loading docks, but as I reached the access road, I spotted a big crowd by the main entrance and a few news vans. There were even police cars. I ditched my bike and walked up, to check it out.

About fifty people were chanting and holding signs.

"Down with NECorp!"

"Stop poisoning our world!"

They sounded tired, like they'd been at it for a while, but were giving it their best shot for the cameras. Some police officers, I think the guy who chased me among them, leaned against their cars, sipping coffee, like it was no big deal.

Jenny was in the crowd. I thought about waving, but she was too far away. Besides, she was busy protesting. Her dad was there, too, the most energetic screamer. I walked toward them until she saw me. She stopped chanting and her face went blank.

When her dad realized she wasn't making any noise, he looked at her and followed her gaze, to me. Then he stopped chanting, too.

Like a little virus passing from person to person, everyone in the crowd stopped chanting and faced me. It was dead silent as the cameras swung in my direction. Someone pointed at me and shouted, "Down with the Corporate Man!"

The rest of them took it up: "Down with the Corporate Man!"

Even Jenny and her dad: "Down with the Corporate Man!"

It was like I *was* NECorp. "Down with the Corporate Man!"

The world was being poisoned, and there wasn't anything they could do about it other than scream. I was furious, too, because I thought there was something I could do about it and it turned out I was wrong. So I shouted back.

I was just sort of yelling at first, not words, just noise. Then I saw one of their signs, *Down with NECorp*, right at my feet, so I leaned down, picked it up and shook it.

"Down with me!!" I screamed. "Down with me!"

And you know what? They stopped shouting and cheered.

So I said, "Down with NECorp!"

They said it back, en masse, "Down with NECorp! Down with NECorp!"

A short woman in a suit shoved a microphone in my face. I thought I recognized her from one of the cable news shows.

"Aren't you Jaiden Beale, the boy adopted by NECorp?"

"Yes."

The crowd was now all chanting behind me, "Down with NECorp!" like they were my backup band.

"Why are you part of this protest? Isn't it biting the hand that feeds you?"

"More like biting the hand that poisons you!" I said.

"But NECorp says their plant produces less mercury than any other in the world."

"They're lying. I saw a confidential memo. They're trying to hide it."

The reporter got all excited. "You saw a memo? Do you have a copy?"

"No . . ."

I was about to explain why when two strong hands appeared on my shoulders. In seconds, I was dragged off. At first I didn't know by whom, then I saw it was Tony, getting me away from the crowd, just like he had at school, only now, against my will. Nancy was beside him.

"Jaiden, don't fight him! We're taking you inside!"

"I don't want to go inside!"

"Are you abusing that boy?" Eric Tate shouted, but a guard shoved him.

Tony pushed me into the lobby. Through the windows I saw security fighting with the protestors. The police rushed up, no longer thinking this was no big deal.

With the doors shut, the sound of the screaming was muffled, but the TV in the lobby was tuned to the station covering the protest, so I could see everyone fighting, and, more importantly, Jenny's dad trying to shield her from the worst of it.

I wanted to rush out and help, but Tony held my arms behind my back. Nancy jammed the call button on the elevator over and over.

It was around then that I realized Ben wasn't going to get his job back, and I was going to wind up in Idaho.

14

MOVING AND SHAKING CAN BE A SEIZURE, TOO

Nancy had been angry about the memo, but this was worse.

"What were you trying to accomplish? Did you want to get kicked out of school? Get me fired? Did you really think you could do any good? How could you be so stupid?"

I sat on my bed as she screamed, but thanks to the magic of video, I was also on the TV screen, saying, "More like biting the hand that poisons you!"

I thought I didn't sound half bad, but hell, I looked awful. My skin was pasty and a few shades whiter than everyone else's.

Tony stood sentry at the door, arms crossed, like a storm trooper. Nancy kept pacing, her face red, her thin, sharp arms gesticulating. She moved those arms so wildly, I was afraid one would just come flying off and her nails would lodge in my face like little daggers and she'd have to use her other arm to yank the first one out.

"Do you even think about the consequences of what you do at all? Ever?"

I knew she wasn't really asking, but I answered, "Yeah, I do. Especially this time. Ted Bungrin already told me if I opened my mouth he'd have me shipped to a foster family." I nodded toward the screen. "I think this counts."

That took some wind out of Nancy's sails. She stretched her back and grabbed her forehead. She looked at the screen and then at me.

"That's crazy. He couldn't have. He wasn't serious, he was . . ."

I widened my eyes. "Oh, he was serious. I wasn't his idea, I was Mr. Hammond's. He said something about antidepressant medication, too."

I wondered about the side effects of that stuff. It's bad enough feeling like a total geek sometimes. I'd hate to turn into a total zombie-geek.

Nancy tried to talk again, but couldn't quite get a sentence out. "But, then why did you . . . Why . . . ?"

I did a by now world-famous shrug. It's a great gesture of surrender.

"I went back to the runoff behind the mall where Ben found me. I saw the junk LiteSpring was pouring into the water."

She got some steam up after that. "And you thought you knew what you were looking at? Scientists and doctors earn a lot of money analyzing things like that and they still disagree. You can't possibly tell if water is dangerous by looking at it!"

"Well, there's this, too."

I pulled back my sleeve to show the bandage on my arm. It was dirty from my night in the woods, but you could still see the wet brown spot in the middle of the cloth.

Both sides of Nancy's lips raised, showing her teeth, not like she was going to bite me or anything, more like she was really worried. The subject suddenly changed.

"Take the bandage off," Nancy said.

With a wince, I peeled the old cotton away. The wound around the stitches was still open. There wasn't blood coming out so much as yellow and green pus. The edge was jagged, and the skin around it looked bruised—brown, blue, and yellow.

It was quite colorful.

"Oh my god," Nancy said. She headed for the door. "You stay there."

I nodded. "Sure. I don't think I could take down Tony anyway in my current weakened condition."

Nancy shook her head and said something I'll never forget: "If you weren't still here, Jaiden, I'd quit right now."

I didn't have the heart to tell her I'd already gotten her fired.

About half an hour later I was taken to the infirmary.

I didn't realize how woozy I was until we started walking there. Eyeballs practically had to prop me up the last fifty yards.

There we met poor, beleaguered Dr. Gespot, who'd once again been summoned from his comfortable home. When we walked in, he was all about getting his examining tools together and complaining, but when he saw my arm, he shut up. He prodded the wound with his cold fingers even though he hadn't put on gloves yet.

"Why didn't you call me sooner?"

"We just looked under the bandage tonight," Nancy said. "Is it serious?"

"I don't know. Let's find out."

First he covered the whole area with a bunch of creamy yellow gunk, then wiped it away. It cleared off all the pus and some of the scab, and didn't hurt much. I guess it was some kind of industrial-strength wound cleaner.

Then he stuck in a few hypodermics. That hurt. Like crazy. I yelled, but he just told me to be quiet. Made me miss the old days when they gave you a lollipop. Anyway, he injected some stuff in there, sucked some other stuff out, and had it rushed off to a lab.

While we waited for the results, he dressed the wound again. We waited around an hour or so before he got a phone call with the lab results. He grunted, asked some questions I couldn't make out, then snapped his phone shut and turned to us.

"Mostly," he said, "We're dealing with an infection, which some stronger antibiotics should take of. You do have small levels of mercury in your blood, though. The muscle aches and joint pain indicate minor poisoning, but you're not showing any major signs of nerve damage or psychological disturbance. Even so, we'll prescribe some dimercaptosuccinic acid, a chelating agent, and get you on that right away."

"What'll that do?" I asked.

"It bonds with any mercury in your system and you'll pass it in your urine."

"Where does it go after that?"

He gave me a look. "Into a soft-drink factory. What do you care as long as it's not in your bloodstream? Just don't swim in any more factory runoffs, eat local fish, or chew on any old thermometers and you should be fine."

He handed me some pills and put on his coat.

"That's it?" I asked. I was a little disappointed.

"That's it. I'll run some more blood tests in a day or so."

"Is it always this easy? Mercury poisoning?"

He shook his head. "Hell no. Mercury can drive you crazy, then kill you."

Did I mention that Emperor Chin went insane and died from drinking this stuff his doctors gave him in an effort to make him immortal? One of the ingredients was mercury.

"You're ridiculously lucky, Jaiden," Dr. Gespot said. Then he left.

I didn't feel lucky. I was glad I wasn't dying, but, really, my life was still over.

Nancy looked relieved, which meant she seemed less tense. She didn't say much more, other than that she'd ask Bungrin how serious he was about what he was going to do to me. She and Tony escorted me back to my room. I was getting escorted a lot these days. It was really late, and we were all exhausted. Nancy left. Tony plopped himself into a chair he'd dragged from a waiting room to a spot outside my door. I crawled into bed.

When morning came, my arm wasn't hurting much, so I got dressed and tried to get some breakfast, but Tony wouldn't let me out. I mean, he blocked the door.

"What about school?" I said.

"No school for you today."

"Nancy around?"

"She's in meetings."

"How long?"

"All day."

That didn't sound good.

"This room is it for you today, so settle in. Maybe, if you behave, you can go to the gym later, but that's all and that's my call."

It was nice, I guess, that Tony had some flexibility in his position.

"I'm hungry."

"Tell me what you want. I'll have it brought up."

"That's okay. I'll call myself."

"You can't. No outgoing calls. No email. They blocked all your accounts. Canceled your cell, too."

"Nancy know about this?"

There was a pause. "Yeah."

"Oh."

I closed the door on him. Hope he didn't take it personally. Wouldn't want to offend the only person in the world with whom I was allowed any contact.

I imagine all kids get grounded sooner or later because they broke some rules, but this was different. Like Ben and Jenny said, these guys were not my parents.

I decided to see if Tony was telling the truth, and it turned out that all of a sudden, out of nowhere, IT decided to get competent. I tried sending an email, but it just sat there in the out-box. I tried using my cell. No signal.

At least the TV still worked. Local news was usually stuck covering store openings and cats in trees, now they were falling all over themselves. It was kind of cute, really. You could see how nervous and excited all the reporters were.

Apparently Jenny's dad assaulted a security guard. He'd been arrested and NECorp was pressing charges. Instead of interviewing someone who was actually there, they had on someone from NECorp, what they call a flak. In this case, Peggy, a woman I knew from

Marketing & PR who used to give me all sorts of swag. I remembered her telling me how much she wanted to be on camera, how she was taking a course on how to be poised.

Well, *someone's* dreams were coming true, because there was Peggy explaining how troubled I'd been ever since they let me attend public school, how I'd fallen in with the wrong crowd, how when NECorp tried to help, I'd run away and been arrested.

When they asked if what I'd said about the memo was true, she explained I was ticked off because NECorp felt it inappropriate to let me watch R-rated movies.

That class paid off. The interviewer tried to catch her off guard, but Peggy stayed on message. I almost believed it myself. I mean, teenagers, what can you do? I tell you, that woman had a great future at NECorp.

Not me. Not so much. Ted had proven true to his word so far (except for that whole mercury poisoning thing). I wondered how long he'd keep me here. Sooner or later I'd get to tell someone my side, how I was being sent to Idaho, just because I tried to tell the truth. Honestly, I have no idea if Idaho is a bad place. I just knew it wasn't here, and Bungrin certainly made it sound bad.

I wish I could tell you that I spent my time in captivity strategizing my escape, or planning how to turn things around, but I didn't do any of that. After I got sick of the news, I turned on my gaming system and spent some time blowing up monsters and aliens. What can I say? It was the only real satisfaction I'd had in ages. Even so, mostly I felt totally defeated.

Around three-thirty, a half hour after school let out, the sky outside my window got that winter-dark tinge, where the edges of the clouds get dimmer and even the air feels kind of heavy. I'd blown a whole day, and wondered how many more just like it were coming.

I was debating whether I should ask Tony to walk me to the gym, when I noticed the Webcam message indicator on my laptop flashing.

"Nate?" I said out loud.

Surprisingly, he answered: "Jaiden! Where the hell you been at, corporate boy?"

The Webcam and mike Nate had helped set up still worked. I clicked open the viewer and found myself staring at his wonderfully chubby cheeks.

"I thought I was shut down! How'd you get past the firewall?"

His face went all smug. "NECorp security is an oxy-moron. I can even change the dinner menu. Why weren't you in school? Everyone was talking about you. Mrs. Shapiro spent the first half of class on civil disobedience. You coming in tomorrow?"

"No. I don't think I am."

"They can't keep you out of school, man. That's like, illegal."

"No, but it looks like they can put me up for adoption in another state."

Nate shook his head, which made him look blurry and pixilated on the screen. "That's cold. Just because you spoke up? That's got to be illegal, too."

"Don't think so. I'm screwed, Nate. Screwed like you wouldn't believe."

"Well, I've got something that will make you feel a little better."

I laughed. "Like what? Did you kidnap Jenny Tate for me or something?"

He waved his hands in front of the camera. "Uh . . . the signal's breaking up."

"What are you talking about? I can see and hear you fine."

"Look, shut up. There's someone here who wants to talk to you," Nate said, then he swiveled his computer and I realized he was trying to spare me some shame. But I couldn't care less, I was so happy. Her face had a bruise on it, but it still looked beautiful.

"Jenny!"

"Hi, Jaiden."

"Where are you guys?"

"Look out your window, toward the woods."

I lifted my laptop and ran to the window. It was getting dark, but behind some trees, I saw Jenny and Nate, waving.

"I didn't know you guys knew each other."

"We didn't until today. I wanted to know how you were doing, so I asked him, but he didn't know, so we thought we'd try to visit. They turned us away. Should have figured that, huh? Then Nate remembered his laptop. Jaiden, I wanted you to know I think what you did yesterday was terribly brave."

"Really stupid, you mean, for all the good it did."

"Yeah, probably that, too, but it was still great."

I noticed the bruise again. "What happened to your face? Was it security?"

"No." An embarrassed smile formed on her face. "My dad. He accidentally clonked me while he was trying to protect me. He's a little overzealous."

"Oh. Ow. Is he out of jail? Does he still hate me?"

"Out on bail and no, not at all. He's completely sorry he forbade me to talk to you. He even spoke to his lawyer about getting you out so you could talk to the press."

My heart skipped a beat. "Really? What did the lawyer say?"

Her face dropped. "He said he didn't think there was anything he could do. You're like . . . NECorp's child. They're entitled to ground you if they feel it's in your best interest. Right now, he's focused on my dad's case, which isn't going well, either."

"So your dad can't do anything about the mercury?"

She shook her head. "He's sure if he did more testing he could prove the levels were out of whack even for the federal guidelines, but now he doesn't have a company. And after the run-in with the police, it's hard to get people together for another protest . . ."

We just looked at each other a minute and she said, out of nowhere, "I miss you."

I was about to say I missed her, too, when the screen filled with Nate's goofy face.

"Jaiden, Jaiden!"

"Hey! I was talking to . . ."

"No, no, listen. If the pollution levels really are that high, NECorp knows it. So what if there are files somewhere that prove it? Where would they keep something like that?"

I shrugged. Nate was sounding all spy movie with the secret file thing. Still, Nancy did pass me that memo, so there was some kind of paper trail. "Bungrin probably keeps all the juicy stuff on his laptop."

"Can you get to it?"

"You mean like steal it? No way. Last I saw it, it was on his desk, about ten feet from him. Besides, he must have half a ton of encryption on that thing. Even if I could get my hands on it, I probably couldn't boot it, let alone open a file."

"I bet I could."

"Yeah, but even if I knocked out Bungrin with my magic sleeping gas and got the laptop, by the time you told me the first line of code, a week would go by."

"Could you sneak us in?"

I heard Jenny's voice chime in. "Yeah! You got me in!"

"Guys, guys! This is a little different. I'm stuck in my room with a guard outside the door and Bungrin never leaves his laptop alone and . . ."

Nate raised his eyebrow. "Really. Just *one* guard?"

15

BREAKING IN ON THE GROUND FLOOR

I admit it. I went through a phase a while ago where I watched tons of old TV shows like *Andy Griffith* and *I Love Lucy*. They're classics for a reason. If you know Lucy, then you know she always comes up with a harebrained scheme to get what she wants and usually drags her poor pal Ethel along for the ride, but not before Ethel puts up a halfhearted effort to get her to listen to reason. Something like, "Lucy, don't you realize what would happen if we got caught?"

Nate was Lucy and I was Ethel. I'm not sure who Jenny was, maybe Fred, who was Ethel's husband, but that doesn't quite work, since she was mostly on Nate's side.

I kept saying it was stupid to try and break in. Security would catch us or Bungrin would make things even worse. Nate was all, "Look, maybe it won't work, but if it does, it'll be completely amazing, and if it doesn't, really, so what? It's not like they'll shoot us. And they've already done as much as they can to you!"

It still felt like some kind of kids' game, like kicking the elevator doors in, or running up and down the halls screaming, but in the end, I couldn't see the downside, except maybe for some breaking and entering charges. Jenny was willing to risk that for the sake of her dad and the world, and Nate was willing to risk it because, well, apparently, my best friend is nuts.

Nate insisted all I had to do was get them up to my room, and he had a "secret plan" (aka harebrained scheme) to handle the rest. I had no idea how we were going to get past Tony, let alone get Bungrin's laptop.

Nate and Jenny left to get some "secret" supplies, agreeing to come back around nine. Bungrin, I knew, would be working late, especially with the company in crisis mode. That gave me a few hours to pace and panic.

Right on time, Nate and Jenny's faces popped back up on my screen. I wasn't going to bother to try to talk Crazy Nate out of it, but I wanted to give Jenny one last chance to back out.

All she said was, "Can we get going? It's freezing out here."

"Okay," I whispered at the screen. "Are you near Receiving?"

Nate swung his Webcam toward the loading docks, bathed in dim yellow security lights. It looked pretty cool, actually, sort of like a video game, a first-person shooter. A solitary security guard paced the rim of the concrete dock, smoking a cigarette. After a minute, he put it out, unlocked one of the doors, and went inside. The little green security car was nowhere in sight, so it was probably on the other side of the building.

"Okay, get behind the big bin on the left," I told them.

I heard scraping and footsteps, then saw a closer view of the dock.

"See the third door? About two years ago, they were bringing in a new desk for Mr. Hammond. It slid off the dolly and smashed that door. That's why it's bent at the bottom. They replaced the lock, but it doesn't sit right. If you lift the handle and yank, it opens."

"Perfect," Nate said.

As they ran across the lot, I saw asphalt moving in a blur. The security lights got brighter as they climbed up to the doors. Then it got dark, but I heard the door jiggle and squeak open.

They were in.

With a dim view of the hallway, I guided them to the freight elevator that led to the hallway outside my office. They hit the button and shortly were on their way up.

Now came the tricky part.

Thinking of how "poised" Peggy was as she lied about me on TV, I put on my game face, went to my door, and opened it. Eyeballs was alone outside, sitting in that lounge chair, nodding off.

"Tony," I said.

His eyes popped open. "What? What's up?"

"Look, I'm sorry, man, this is really stupid. But I thought you should know."

He sprang to his feet and walked over. "What? What's stupid?"

"I told them not to come up, but they wouldn't listen."

His brow got all furrowed. "Huh? Who's coming up?"

I tried as hard as I could to make it sound like it wasn't a big deal. "Some friends of mine. They just wanted to see me, so they're sneaking in through the freight elevator."

He looked at me. "Right. Nice try. This place is locked up."

"No, really. I just don't want them to get in trouble. If they get here, could you not turn them in? Maybe just walk them out again?"

He rolled his eyes. "Jai-man! How could you even know they're coming? You're sealed off."

I gave him a famous shrug. "My pal Nate's got this Web-cam thing and he got past the firewall, and . . ."

Eyeballs was about to explain again how that was not possible, when the freight elevator doors opened and Jenny and Nate came out, all grins.

"Jaiden!" Nate roared and he started trucking down the hall toward me and Tony in this exaggeratedly happy march.

"Holy crap," Eyeballs said. He reached for his cell.

I put my hand on the phone and tried to get all wide-eyed and innocent. "Tony, I told you! Please, don't get them in trouble. Come on, man, just walk them back down."

By then, Nate was right there with us and Jenny was coming up fast.

Tony pulled the phone from me. Nate started talking, fast.

"Hey, look, look, look, Jaiden's my best friend, can't you let us visit him for five minutes? Five minutes?"

Tony shook his head. "No way. I'm calling security on your asses right now."

"Couldn't you just walk them down yourself?"

"And leave you up here alone? No way, 007."

Nate pretended to get all pissed. "You suck. I just wanted five freaking minutes."

"Yeah, and you're going to get five freaking years in a youth camp," Tony said.

No sooner did he flip open his phone then Nate's arm came out and up and he jammed something that looked like a black remote-control unit into Anthony's neck.

There was a quick buzzing sound, like an electric razor. All of a sudden, Tony's eyeballs rolled back into his head and he fell to the ground like a big stuffed doll.

I was in total shock.

Nate jumped up and down, voice cracking as he talked. "It worked! It worked! My Taser worked! Ha! Oh yeah, oh yeah! I can't believe I got this thing on eBay! Freak, yeah!"

He looked at a little dial on it. "And I've got two charges left! Yes!"

Jenny's reaction was similar to mine, but with her own spin. She started screaming, "You killed him! You killed him!"

Hearing this, Nate tried to hush her. "Shh! Shh! No, no! It's okay! It's okay! He's fine! He's fine! He'll wake up in less than an hour!"

She put her own hands over her mouth to stop herself screaming, but then she took to shaking and making this little whimpering noise.

"Nate, are you totally out of your mind?" I said. "This is assault! Now what are we going to do?"

"What do you think? Shut up and help me drag him inside!"

He bent over and pulled at Tony. Tony, built like a linebacker, did not move.

Nate looked at me and Jenny, furious. He picked up Tony's cell and shoved it in our faces. "Help me drag him inside, or call Security yourself! One minute it's we've got to do the right thing, then, when you actually *do* something, it's all oh dear, did we hurt someone? Please. Give me a break."

This was Nate aka Chipmunk Cheeks, the guy with buckteeth. I guess you never really know someone until you're breaking and entering with them.

"So, Nate," I said. "Ever kill a man?"

"Not yet," he said with a weird grin.

The three of us dragged Tony into my room. Nate pulled some extension cords out of his backpack and we used those to tie his hands and legs. Then he pulled out some duct tape and wrapped a piece around Tony's mouth.

"Can he breathe though that?" Jenny asked, worried.

"I think so."

"You *think* so?" I said.

Nate rolled his eyes, put a strip of duct tape across his own mouth and breathed a few times through his nose. Then he pulled it off and winced.

"See? He can breathe. Okay?"

When Tony was secured, Nate looked around. "This your room? Like the desk."

"Can we get on with the secret plan, please?" I said.

We rolled Tony to the side of my bed, so he'd be hard to see if anyone walked in. I covered him with a blanket and Jenny put a pillow under his head. Nate shook his head.

Then we went back out into the hall.

"This freight elevator doesn't go to the top floor, so the fastest way up is the main elevator," I said, and we got moving.

Since it was after business hours, half the lights were out, so it was dark enough to hide and quiet enough to hear if anyone was coming.

The first problem we faced was that once you're in the

main halls, they're long, really long, like the length of the building, so if someone happened to be working late, or the cleaning crew was around, they'd see you a mile away. We tiptoed along, like a trio of idiot spy kids from one of those crappy movies, wondering how long our luck would hold out.

It did for a while. We made it to the elevator, the one with the door I'd kicked in, but when I pressed the Up button, it didn't light up like it was supposed to.

"Maybe the bulb's out," Jenny suggested.

"No," I said. "When it's this quiet, you'd hear it moving in the shaft."

I leaned my head against the door, looking at the dent I'd left in it, and listened. Nothing. That's when I noticed something new; a magnetic stripe reader. You could tell it was a rush job. It didn't even line up with the edge of the elevator buttons.

"What the hell is that?" I said.

"You don't know?" Jenny asked.

"I do," Nate said. He had his laptop out and was trying to balance it against the wall as he typed. The bulky thing nearly fell out of his hands twice as he worked.

"*Had* to give Caitlin the PDA, right?"

"Shut up!" He typed some more. "This is easy. They haven't even encrypted the WiFi, so I'm already in the system." He stopped typing and started scanning the screen. "I've got a memo released today. They installed a new security system because of the protests. You need a card to use the elevators."

I exhaled. "If we use the stairs, we'll set off the alarms. That's it. We're done."

"No! We knocked Tony out! There has to be a way up there!" Jenny protested.

I didn't want to disappoint her; I didn't want to disappoint myself. Hell, I didn't even want to disappoint Nate, but I couldn't think of anything.

Meanwhile, Crazy Nate was typing away like he was playing a video game. "Okay, I've got the maintenance maps. We're here, and if we head down to the coffee area, we should be able to climb into the ventilation shaft and make our way upstairs."

"Give it up, James Bond! We're going to go crawling in ventilation shafts now?"

"Why not?" he said. He actually looked a little hurt. "They do it in movies."

In for a penny, in for a pound, so we followed "Lucy" down to the coffee area. It was a ten-by-ten-foot room with a sink, a fridge, a coffee machine, and yes, the terminal for a ventilation shaft. I climbed onto the counter and tried pulling off the grid, but my fingers couldn't quite pry the thing off. Jenny handed me a butter knife, which did the trick nicely. The cover popped off and I gently laid it behind the sink.

"We follow that shaft about a hundred feet, then it should head up," Nate said.

They took off their bulky coats and I shoved them into

the hole ahead of us, in case they needed to exit fast. Jenny climbed up next to me and I helped her in. I went in second and Nate brought up the rear.

There are three important differences between real-life ventilation shafts and the ones you see in the movies. First, real ones are smaller. We had a terrible time squirming through the damn thing. Second, they're not one solid piece. They're a series of pieces welded together, and whenever we snaked over a seam, we either cut our clothes or scraped our skin. There was lots of tearing and wincing as we made our way.

Third, and most important, real-life ventilation shafts are not made to hold the weight of a human being. What they're made to hold, and what they hold very well, is air. And air isn't very heavy at all.

Looking back, I'm surprised we made it as far as we did, which was about eight feet into the next room. Then there was this crunching sound, like a soda can being crushed.

Nate said, "Wait . . ." like he'd had a new brilliant idea, but then the section of the shaft we were in tore loose and tumbled down.

The fall itself, about eight feet, was really quick. I guess it was better we didn't see it coming, but I wouldn't say that that made it any less painful. Hitting the ground hurt like hell. The only thing that didn't hurt was my wounded arm, which was now healing nicely.

My head rang and my eyesight blurred, but I managed

to push aside the broken pieces of shaft and make out that not only were we in a small office, but that someone was there, working late. Well, they weren't working at all right then, because they were too busy staring at us. It took a second for me to focus and realize who it was.

Nancy.

Who else would be working late on a Friday?

I didn't know whether to be relieved or upset.

She spoke first. "What are you doing?" she asked.

Simple enough question. I wiped some dust from my mouth and said, "We were trying to break into Bungrin's office, to see if we could steal any files off his laptop that proved the pollution was worse than he's admitting, but there's some kind of new security system on the elevators."

"Dude! You gave away the secret plan!" Nate said.

I tried to respond calmly. "Dude, I think falling out of the ceiling did that."

Nancy opened her desk drawer and pulled a little silver bottle out. I think it was what they call a hip flask. She spun the cap off, took a slug, then turned back to us.

"How'd you get past Anthony?"

Nate grinned. "Taser!"

She took another, longer slug, which I think drained the bottle. I, for one, was not going to listen to her lecture about substance abuse in the same way anymore. Anyway, she put the bottle down and looked at us again.

"Jaiden, as of five o'clock this afternoon, you officially

are no longer my responsibility. So . . ." She straightened her skirt, stood up, and started walking past us toward the door. "In my purse, there's a security card that operates the elevators. I am going to go get some coffee. I'll be about twenty minutes. When I report this strange mess in my office, I intend to pretend I didn't see you. Do not tell anyone I said this, but if you do manage to use your Taser on Ted Bungrin, try to shove it in his crotch."

Then she left.

Shaking the dust from my head I stood and started rifling her purse.

"I think I should call my father," Jenny said. "This has gotten way out of hand."

Nate and I both turned to her and said, "No!" loud enough to make her wince.

I couldn't believe how much stuff Nancy kept in there and how badly organized it was. It was like this person who was totally anal about everything else had this one little pocket of utter chaos in her life. After about a minute, I put my hands on a thick white plastic card with the NECorp logo on it.

"Got it! Let's go."

Jenny gave me a look.

"What?" I asked.

She stood there stiffly. "I'm not an idiot or a wuss for wanting to call my dad, you know. I got arrested during the protest for standing up for what I believe in."

I stared at her. "You're right. I'm sorry. It's just with Nancy gone, Nate's right. There's nothing else they *can* do to me, nothing to lose. You don't have to come, though."

"I want to. I'm just scared."

Nate stomped his feet. "Guys, either get a room or let's get going!"

As we walked back to the elevators, junk from the ceiling and ventilation shaft came off our shoes and we left a kind of white, crunchy trail. When someone from the cleaning staff appeared far down the hall, I thought we were done for, but we just leaned into the wall, and after a second he went into another office.

I swiped the card through the reader and the light came on. In a few seconds, we were heading up. As we shared those awkward moments in the elevator with nothing else to do but sweat, Jenny turned to Nate and asked, "So what do we do when we find Bungrin?"

He held up his Taser and smiled.

"Could you not take that thing out unless you're going to use it?" I asked. "Never mind. Quiet. We're here."

The damaged doors wobbled as they opened. We crept out. Jenny and Nate got their first look at the waiting room with its gallery and flowing river.

"It's so disgusting," Jenny said. "What a waste of space and energy!"

But I could tell Nate thought it was cool.

We walked toward the giant doors to Bungrin's office.

The waiting room was dim, making a thin line of light under the doors easily visible.

"He's here," I whispered.

"Great. How do we get him out and into the hands of . . ."—he raised the Taser again and narrowed his eyes—"The Eliminator?"

"I've got an idea. Give me your coats."

They were thick winter coats, just big enough to cover the small space along the stream between the waiting room and the office. Shortly the water outside dried up, which meant the water inside would back up and pour all over Bungrin's nice clean carpet. I figured that'd send him stumbling out in a fit.

We ducked behind Cheryl Diego's desk and waited. We didn't have long. In seconds, the black doors swung inward and old Ted, shirtsleeves rolled up and an annoyed expression on his usually placid face, stormed out. He stood right in front of the desk, so close, we could see his shiny shoes, the perfect laces, the perfect socks.

Nate looked at me. I nodded, lifted the finely pleated pants leg, and watched as Nate zapped the CEO of NECorp. Bungrin went down faster than Anthony. Probably because he weighed less.

This time Jenny didn't scream, she just smiled. What was not to like?

We dragged his no-longer moving-and-shaking body back inside the office. The pneumatic doors closed silently behind us. Water pooled on the floor from the backed-up stream, but there was no time to deal with that now. The prize was open and waiting for us on the aircraft-carrier-sized desk—Bungrin's laptop, already booted.

Nate giggled as he ran up to it and started clicking keys like crazy.

"It's locked, it's locked . . . wait, I'm in!"

I went up to the water wall and stared at it. Jenny stepped up beside me and leaned into me a bit. "So this is your home, huh?"

I shook my head. "It's just a house. Not even a house. Well, you know what I mean."

She nodded and we watched the water until Nate squealed, "I don't believe it!"

We raced to look at the screen. Nate pointed at a bunch of memos and charts. "Those mercury filter-thingies were safe even if you tripled production, but Bungrin pushed them harder, and every time one fails it doesn't just stop working, it dumps all the mercury it collected back in the water, *twenty* times the legal limit."

"Holy crap," I said. "That's it. That's our smoking gun."

"Here's the part where you get down on your knees, on your *knees*, Jaiden, and thank the stars for Caitlin, because you know what my laptop has that Bungrin's machine and my PDA do not?"

"What?"

He tapped a little black slot on the side of his machine.

"DVD burner. I connect the computers, make a copy of his files, and Bungrin won't even realize what we've got until it's too late."

We looked over at his still form, lying on the carpet.

With a grin, Nate added, "Maybe he'll even think he just fell or something."

"Fine. Do it."

"Thank Caitlin."

"Thank you, Caitlin."

"Who's Caitlin, anyway?" Jenny asked. "Caitlin Fermelli?"

I shook my head. "Tell you later."

Burning a whole DVD takes a while, and looking back, I wish Nate had just picked a few files to copy. I kept thinking someone would come through those two big black doors to arrest us.

After waiting forever, I asked, "How much longer?"

He waved me off. "Almost there."

Getting antsy, I looked in the spot where Bungrin's body was supposed to be. Only, it wasn't.

"Nate! Nate!" I said.

"Almost . . ."

Just as he whipped a silver DVD out of his laptop's slot, I yanked his shoulder. He turned to me with this look of total triumph. "It's totally burned, baby! We're out of here!"

I almost didn't have the heart to tell him. "Bungrin's gone."

I felt Jenny tapping on my shoulder.

"No, he's not, Jaiden," she said.

I turned and saw she was right. There was Bungrin, standing in the opposite corner of the office, looking fit as a fiddle.

And he was holding a gun.

16

YOURS FOR THE MULTITASKING

Any illusions we might have had that Bungrin probably wouldn't actually use a gun against a trio of
wacky and lovable kids went right out the window when
he fired at us.

I knew from TV that a real gun didn't sound or work
like one from a video game, but that didn't really prepare
me for this. There was a sharp crack like a splintering piece
of wood and Nate's Taser, which sat on the desk just a few
inches from the edge of his laptop, exploded. I mean, it utterly dusted. One second, slick black Taser, the next, plastic shards flying in the air.

There was also this weird little time lag that's hard to
describe; you're watching the gun fire, hearing the sound,
seeing the Taser disintegrate all in slow motion. For a flash,
you're removed from it, thinking, huh, that's not so bad, it
couldn't possibly have anything to do with me, but then out
of nowhere, the rest of your body catches up with what

you're seeing and your glands start pouring tons of adrenaline into your body and you realize you might die at any second.

I ran, away from Bungrin. Jenny gasped and did the same. Neither of us made a sound, but Nate screamed in a weird way that sounded like a cross between a little girl and a wounded puppy. The DVD still in his hand, he dove behind the desk. I don't think Nate was bravely trying to protect the DVD because it had the information we'd risked it all for, I think he'd just forgotten he was holding it.

I still couldn't believe what was going on. I started thinking maybe Bungrin was this incredible marksman and he was just trying to eliminate a threat and scare us by hitting the Taser, but then he said, "Crap! I missed," real loudly, fired again, and hit the corner of the desk.

"Are you crazy?" I screamed.

Bungrin turned my way and said, "You tell me."

He glanced at his watch. "Time's up!"

I jumped as he fired again. I don't know where that bullet went, I was too busy eating carpet, but near as I could tell, it didn't hit me. I rolled over on my back and saw him coming toward me.

Out of the corner of my eye, I saw Jenny grab a laptop from the desk and race out the door.

Good, I thought. She made it. Not so good that Bungrin was walking up to me with a gun in his hand. As he came forward, I kind of skittered backward like a spider, hand-walking on the wet floor until my head bumped the bottom of the fountain. Water sloshed onto my hair and forehead from the overflow.

I heard this weird slurping sound and all of a sudden the overflow stopped, but I was too worried about the crazy man with the gun to wonder what it was. I wiped the water from my eyes to see him towering over me, aiming the gun at my head.

"Some of the protestors threatened violence, so Security suggested I start carrying a weapon. I was knocked out. When I came to, I thought it was a kidnapping, I thought my life was in danger, so I fired to defend myself. By the time I realized it was you, it was too late," he said. He said it like he was practicing his story for the press, but really I think he just wanted me to know he'd be fine even if he did kill me.

I was going to ask how he planned to explain the fact that he didn't recognize me even though he'd shot me point-blank in the face, then I realized he could just say it was dark, or he was confused. But really I couldn't get past the whole I-was-about-to-die thing enough to speak.

Then out of nowhere, this big black blob fell on top of his head and shoulders. Bungrin stumbled back, gurgled and tried to rip it off, but it was very heavy and, judging from the drops of water that flew from it, very wet.

"Jaiden, come on!" Jenny screamed.

As she helped me get to my feet, I realized what had happened. She hadn't just run off. She'd grabbed the soaked coats from the stream and tossed them on Bungrin's head. I was going to say thanks, but with Bungrin almost free of the coats, it seemed more important to run.

As we headed for the door, I screamed at Nate. He did this funky running crawl out from behind the desk. I had no idea anyone could crawl that fast, but by the time he was at the door, he'd used his arms to push himself to his feet. The disk was still clenched in his hand.

We nearly tripped over our soggy feet as we hit the hall and booked. Nate, who was drier, actually got ahead of me and Jenny. As soon he reached the elevators, he started jamming the Down button like crazy with his index finger.

As if that would help.

As I passed, I grabbed him by the shoulder and yanked him along. The staircase was a few yards away. All three of us pushed through the door at once, which set off the alarm. Instead of the wild screech I was hoping for, there was this really low beeping sound. I figured, hoped really, it was connected to the rest of the NECorp security system, which would mean it was only a question of time before someone came up and saved us from getting killed. I mean, unless they were all part of Bungrin's secret zombie army now, which, if you stop to think about it, isn't nearly as strange as the fact that the CEO of a major corporation was trying to kill three teenagers with a handgun.

With the down staircase right in front of us, for some sick reason my best buddy Nate turned and headed for the stairs that led to the roof.

"Down!" I screamed. Then I pointed at the freaking stairs, like he couldn't see them.

"Up!" he screamed back. And he pointed, too.

"Down! It's the only way out!" I said, like it wasn't the most obvious thing in the world.

"Up! He'll never think to look for us that way!"

I really didn't want to get into a major, no-holds-barred argument with Nate, and it didn't look like Jenny was going to break the deadlock anytime soon. She just stood there with the laptop in her hand, staring at us as we yelled at each other, like we were nuttier than Bungrin. Realizing that in a few seconds the rootin' tootin' excc would be upon us and it wouldn't matter which direction we went if we didn't go somewhere, I caved and we headed up.

After two flights of steel and concrete steps, we slammed into another emergency door, heard another alarm beeping, and spilled out into the eerie stillness of the night.

Once we were all through the door, standing on this red gravel that covered everything, Nate pushed it shut. Surprisingly the beeping stopped. Or, maybe we couldn't hear it anymore with the door closed.

Nate was panting. Little bursts of water vapor shot out of his mouth as he talked. "Okay, okay. Now we just wait here. No way is he going to find us. No way."

I looked around. I'd lived at the NECorp headquarters my entire life, but you know, I'd never been up on the roof. I felt like someone who lived in Manhattan, but never bothered to see the Statue of Liberty. The first thing I noticed, what with me being wet from the floor and not having a coat on, was that it was freaking freezing.

The second thing I noticed was that the view was nice. There was a dull haze from the lights in the parking lot, but if you looked straight up you could see tons of stars. As my eyes adjusted to the gloom, I could make out the houses in the development where my fake house was and the football field outside of Deever High. In the other direction I saw the strip mall, the woods, and what I thought was the top of the LiteSpring factory.

It wasn't the whole world exactly, but, in a nutshell, it was mine.

Jenny, meanwhile, had the laptop open and was typing furiously, which seemed odd under the circumstances, until she explained.

"I left my cell in my coat," she said. "So I'm emailing my dad and everyone I know. I can even send them the data straight from Bungrin's laptop."

"Only one problem with that," Nate said.

"What?"

"That's not Bungrin's laptop. That one's mine."

Jenny looked at the rig, confused, then said, "Oh yeah."

"Don't sweat it, we've still got this," Nate said, his breathing slowing down. He held his hand up and showed the DVD.

I took it from him, looked at the rainbow shine on the data side, and actually thought for a minute there that we'd won.

I started walking over to Jenny with it, so she could send the data, when I noticed she was shivering. So, I put my soggy arm around her.

"See that? You are cool," I said.

"No, I'm not," she answered. "I'm f-f-freezing."

Nate saw us and rolled his eyes again, then he started looking around, like he was trying to find another way down or out, but really, I think, he was just trying to avoid looking at us. Then he got this weird expression and started walking toward us.

"Jaiden, there's something I really gotta tell you. There was a lot of stuff on that laptop that I copied over to the DVD. Bungrin's not just . . ."

Before Nate could finish, the door to the roof swung open and I realized how stupid I was for expecting Security to show up and save us because of the lame beeping alarm.

It wasn't Security, of course, it was Bungrin.

"No!" Nate screamed. Not like he was terrified or anything, just like he was really, really annoyed. "No, no, no! Why'd you come up here? What made you think we were here?"

Bungrin raised an eyebrow. "It was easy. There's all this water and white crap on your feet. As soon as I retraced my steps and looked down, I just followed the footprints."

Nate lifted his sneaker, like Bungrin had some reason to lie about it, then tossed his head up and rolled his eyes. "Damn!"

All this time, Jenny was inching farther away, toward some kind of air-conditioning unit. I thought for a second she might make a run for it, but Bungrin just pointed his gun at her. "No, no, back here now."

Jenny, looking like a deer caught in the headlights, obediently walked over next to me and Nate.

Bungrin looked at his fancy-ass wristwatch, typically impatient. "Okay, hand over that DVD and the laptop."

Jenny looked at him, real defiant. "Because you know that plant is poisoning the water, right? Because you know you've been lying about the mercury levels? And then you're going to just . . . kill us?"

Bungrin looked surprised for a moment, not so much at what she was saying, but at the fact that she was talking at all. Once he got over that, which took maybe a half second, he nodded vigorously and said, "Uh . . . yeah! That's pretty much it," like she'd said two and two was four.

He came closer. It was one of those lose-lose situations, you know? Maybe if we'd trained for weeks and had some sort of tight attack plan, we could take him off balance, maybe even get the gun. He was big, not as big as Tony, but our one real weapon, the Taser, was gone, so there was nothing we could do.

There I was, standing there with the DVD, the proof we needed right in my hand. Bungrin had already proven he was willing to shoot us, and it looked like whatever patience he'd had, which was never much to speak of, was gone.

But then I realized, what the hell? If you're on a roller coaster to hell, you might as well put your hands up and scream. Maybe I couldn't do anything with the DVD, but maybe someone else could.

While Bungrin glared at me, I flung the silver disc out into the night sky, like a Frisbee. It headed out like a flying saucer, over the parking lot.

Nate and Jenny grinned. Bungrin looked shocked a moment, but then, in a flash, he raised the gun, aimed, and fired.

And the son of a bitch hit it.

Scores of little silver pieces danced in the air, turning end over end like some polyethylene plastic rain.

"Oh, man!" screamed Nate. "Oh, man! That really, really *sucks*!"

Jenny's face just dropped.

As for Bungrin, well, he looked about as surprised as we did.

"That's it then, eh?" He took a few steps closer to me. "Turn around, Jaiden, it makes for a better story if I can't see you from the front."

"You're going to shoot us anyway?" I said.

"Yeah, now you really do know too much, yada yada yada. Turn around."

"What if I say no?"

"I'll shoot your girlfriend first."

I thought about that scene with Clint Eastwood, the bad guy, and Clint's daughter. This was kind of like that, only I didn't have a gun, like Clint did, so there wasn't much I could do. I looked at Jenny a second, thinking I'd never see her or anything else again, then I did like he asked and turned my back to him.

I could see the stars mixing with bits of DVD dust. I had no idea where the gun was, if it was by his side, pointed at my back, or right up against the hair on my head. I felt him get closer, though, I felt him lean in nice and close so he could whisper.

"Just to make things absolutely clear to you, even without me in the mix, it never would have worked your way. NECorp could never have come clean and shut down the LiteSpring plant. It'd be suicide."

"How do you know?" I asked. Sure he was smart about business, but what was he, Nostradamus or something?

"Because," he said. "We tried it, and I saw what happened."

"What? What do you mean?"

"We tried it. With SafeWarm. One bad valve, one stinking bad valve nearly brought all of NECorp down. It took ages to recover from that. Ages. Ages for NECorp, ages for me. And what did we get for all our troubles? You."

226

I turned around and looked at him. The gun was out, held level at about his waist. He had that smile as usual, but his eyes were wavering in their sockets, like there was some kind of pressure building behind them and steam was about to come whistling out of his ears.

"What did you have to do with it? Dan Blake was the plant manager, and he got fired."

Nate called out, his voice all shaky. "He *is* that Dan Blake guy, Jaiden. He just changed his name. Some of his stock holdings are still in his old name."

Bungrin whirled toward Nate. "You're a smart one, aren't you? Yeah, that's it. Hide in plain sight. I'm Dan Blake. That one stupid valve set back my career ten years. I had to change my name and start over."

He turned back to me, really angry, like it was my fault my parents died. "You know how much time that cost me? I should've been retired by now, sitting on my yacht with my trophy wife and all the toys in the world. Instead, here we are. For the want of a nail, the war was lost. Almost."

Well, you can probably guess that I was pretty surprised. I didn't have any real-life experiences to measure the feeling against, but there were lots of examples from comic books. It was like when Batman found out the Joker killed his parents, or Spider-Man found out that the crook he failed to stop went on to shoot his uncle Ben. I was so full of fear and rage, I really felt entitled to turn into some kind of superhero.

How great would it have been if I could've reached out, lifted Bungrin up, and thrown him halfway across the city, where he could crash through the wall of his polluted factory and land in a pile of radioactive poisonous gunk, and all the mercury could pour out of the river, right into his mouth?

Remember what I said about the roller coaster to hell? I couldn't actually hurl him or anything, but I figured I'd give it a shot.

I pulled back and punched him in the stomach. It felt like I was hitting a thick, firm mattress. No give at all. He just laughed.

"Really, Beale. That the best you got?"

I hauled off and clocked him in the jaw. That gave a little. His whole head turned to the left.

"Remember what Nancy said!" Nate screamed.

So I kneed him in the crotch.

That hurt. I could tell, because his mouth turned into a little circle and he bent forward. With his head all of a sudden close to me, I punched him in the jaw again.

"Yeah, Jaiden!" Nate said.

On the one hand, it felt pretty good. On the other, I didn't really feel like I was accomplishing much of anything. It wouldn't bring back my parents, and he was still holding the gun.

When I grabbed for that, he just threw me. I went up in the air, landed hard, and skidded across the gravel.

I looked up and he leveled the gun at me. He hadn't even broken a sweat.

"Sideways is just as good," he said. Then he glanced at

his watch one last time. "Now, time is really up," he said as he aimed.

The door to the roof burst open, filling the night air with that lame beeping sound. It was Tony, with a bunch of NECorp security running up behind him, come to rescue us.

No, really.

I felt even better as they all swarmed out and made a semicircle around me, Bungrin, Nate, and Jenny. Better yet, their guns were out, but they weren't pointed at us. They were pointed at Bungrin.

One of the security guys nodded at old Ted. "Mr. Bungrin, could you please put down the gun?"

Bungrin's perfect smile burst on his face. He held the gun out by the handle and one of the guards grabbed it. "About time you got here," he said, then he nodded toward us. "They broke in, attacked me in my office, and tried to steal company secrets."

"That's a lie!" Nate screamed.

Bungrin ignored him. "Anthony, take Mr. Beale back to his room and hand the other two over to the police. I will be pressing charges."

Tony shook his head. "I don't think so."

Bungrin's eyes narrowed. "Who paid you to think?"

"I know it's not in my contract, Mr. Bungrin, but you can call it an added benefit," Tony said. "The cops are on their way, and they're coming to arrest you."

All of a sudden Bungrin's game face got all twisted,

like he was ordering himself to keep smiling, but the message kept getting lost on the way to his brain because it was getting mixed in with all kinds of totally unwanted feelings, like smugness, disgust, and confusion.

"What? What are you talking about?"

"We saw the whole thing, heard your confession," Tony said.

"Confession? What do you . . ." He looked around. "That's not possible. There are no security cameras up here," he said.

That's when Jenny, who I'd thought had just been all quiet and scared all this time, quietly cleared her throat. I heard her, but no one else did, so she said, "ahem" as loud as she could. Everyone turned around.

She held up Nate's laptop and pointed to the little button-sized Webcam on top. "There's one camera, and a mike, right here. Nate left the security window open, so I sent the feed there, to my dad, to the local press, and directly onto the Web where it's already being enjoyed by"—she checked the screen—"eighty-two viewers!"

If the whole scene wasn't enough like the movies for you, just then the sound of police sirens filled the air. Bungrin's face, right on cue, went all white and blank like he finally knew he was toast, like he finally knew it was really over.

I walked right up to Jenny, amazed, and said, "You are so cool!"

"Yes," she said with a little smile. "I am."

17

POSTTRUTH

There's this comedian from the 1950s, Lenny Bruce, who said that satire equals tragedy plus time, meaning if you wait long enough, even the saddest thing will seem funny. So, I don't know, maybe in thirty years these past few weeks of my life, during which I met my first girlfriend, almost got arrested, got mercury poisoning, and got shot at, will all be a major laugh riot.

But if that's really true, wouldn't stuff like World War II or Shakespeare's *King Lear* be absolutely hysterical by now?

Around a week or so later, I was lying in bed, having this dream about what it'd be like when I got out of NECorp and finally got my forty million dollars. I was buying everything I could see, games, DVDs, books, cars, until, sometime after I got the jet pack, I ran out of things I wanted.

This made me all philanthropic and I started hiring

scientists to cure diseases, which of course they hadn't done before only because no one paid them enough. This act of great benevolence made me terribly famous. There was major gratitude from all sorts of hot girls whose lives had been saved courtesy of my great big pile of money.

Just as I was running out of cash, people everywhere, all across the globe, stopped believing in money. It became totally worthless, and everyone started singing "All You Need Is Love" by the Beatles. It's this really cool song about how you can't do anything impossible, because once you do it, it's not impossible anymore.

The song, of course, turned out to be the tune my new iPod alarm was playing. By the time I shook the dream and realized I was neither free nor did I own a jet pack, I remembered I had an appointment with the new CEO, to "discuss my future."

I had no idea what that meant.

After school, though, I planned to meet up with Jenny, Nate, and Caitlin and see *Hell Is Calling*, a cool new action movie involving a series of interdimensional vortices created by a demon-possessed cell-phone ringtone. It was our first big night out after all the excitement, and I wanted to look decent, so I put on some new jeans before heading to the cafeteria.

It was early, so there was no line between me and Ben. You'd think it would feel great having him back, but it was awkward. Oh, his first day he did tell me that I'd done great, but once he was back in the grind, I think he was feeling trapped.

Trapped at NECorp. Now there's a feeling I can certainly empathize with.

I wanted to make him feel better, and I was still thinking about my dream, so as I took my eggs, bacon, and home fries, I said, "You know, when I get my money, you can totally blow this joint."

"And work for *you*?" he said. He got this look on his face, not angry, but kind of hurt. I realized maybe it was embarrassing for him to be rescued from his mundane life by some dumb kid who'd be rich by accident. I also noticed we weren't standing eye to eye anymore. I'd shot up maybe an inch in the last few weeks. I was taller than he was.

Maybe that hurt, too.

I shook my head. "I was thinking we'd be partners, set up some kind of business. You already do a better job running *this* place than the guys in charge."

He twisted his head and looked at me some more. "We could open a diner?"

"A chain. It's a crime to keep home fries like these a secret."

He smiled. There was this trace of bitterness to it, but it was still a smile. He shook his head, then smiled again, this time right at me, without the bitter part.

"Thanks, Jaiden," he said. "I'll keep that in mind."

I headed off to find a table. Nancy was by herself, typing

away. As I passed, still typing with one hand, she raised the other to wave at me. I waved back, but knew better than to join her when she was busy. She was promoted to SVP and had been happily working her head off ever since.

I sat down, thinking about how so few people loved their jobs and so many more hated them. To be fair, I knew miserable executives and happy cleaning people, but the executives were miserable on their yachts and the cleaning people were happy despite not having health insurance. I like to think, though, that a sick maniac like Bungrin would be miserable no matter where he was and no matter how much money he did or didn't have.

It was still utterly cool to think about how he was arrested that night. Despite his high-paid lawyers, Bungrin totally wound up with his evil ass in jail. Mostly it was thanks to Jenny and this really nice shot she got of old Ted waving his gun around and agreeing with her that he'd lied to everyone about the mercury levels.

That clip was number one on YouTube for six freaking weeks. Heh-heh.

NECorp was forced into ultra-apology mode. LiteSpring was shut down, the deal to buy JenCare canceled. Eric Tate was rehired and put in charge of remediating the water, with NECorp footing the bill. They had to. Power of the press. Power of the people.

It couldn't have gone better, except maybe for one thing. A replacement for Bungrin had to be found quickly, and, after hours of intense, behind-closed-doors arguing, there was only one person the board could agree on.

After breakfast, I swiped my personal key card through the security slot, waited for the wobbly elevator door to open, and headed to the top floor. The fake stream was flowing again through the waiting room, and a cheerful Cheryl Diego ushered me in. She asked if I wanted a soda or something, then disappeared behind those huge double doors.

The first thing I noticed was that some of the carpet had been removed, probably so it wouldn't get moldy, but the water wall was still working fine. The guy standing in front of it, Desmond Hammond III, seemed likewise no worse for wear.

You just can't keep a good crazy person down.

He didn't say hello, he just nodded toward his water wall. "You know, Jaiden, for the first time in ages, I spent two days at home. It's a big place. Lots of rooms, and a huge lake out back. I spent some time by that lake, looking at the surface of the water, thinking how different it was from my water wall here. It had twigs in it, and all sorts of other junk, just floating around willy-nilly. Quite honestly, I didn't care for it one bit."

His face got all serious, and he turned to me. "I wouldn't be back if it wasn't for you, and I want you to know I am so sorry about what happened."

"I know," I said.

"You do realize we're not *all* like Ted Bungrin, don't you?"

I shrugged. "Oh, sure. Of course not."

Some of you, after all, don't have guns.

"Things will be different, I promise. We'll take our hit on LiteSpring but we'll survive. We always do. We're part of the fabric of the world economy, a hand in everything. NECorp, even if its name changes, can't ever really die. And we'll just keep growing. Sooner or later, we'll even have a stake in that lake behind my house. I'm not certain how it will happen, but it will."

He smiled and turned back to his wall. "I have a story for you, to explain why I called you here today. There was this factory in Japan where production declined, below quota. While trying to figure out why, one of the foremen thought perhaps the light was too dim for the workers, so he had brighter bulbs installed. Productivity shot up, but after awhile, it dropped off again. Suspecting the light had something to do with it, he reinstalled the dimmer bulbs, expecting productivity to go down even further. To his surprise, productivity shot up, then dropped off again. So, he just started switching the bulbs every two weeks, first dimmer, then brighter. Finally, productivity stayed up. Do you know what that taught him?"

That people are strange? I thought, but I said, "No. What?"

"That people respond when they think someone's

paying attention, that someone cares. Which brings us to you. You're what, fourteen now?"

"Yes sir."

"Four years and you'll be off to college, pretty much a man, on your own."

"I guess."

"There's been a lot of talk lately that NECorp hasn't done right by you, that maybe a corporation isn't the right structure in which to nurture a human being. As a result, there's been serious discussion that you might be better off in a more traditional family."

He stuck his finger into the flowing water of the wall, making an upside-down V, just like Bungrin had. "Much as I've always thought of you as a son, one of the things I realized as I stared at that filthy lake during my two days of unemployment, is that I'm really not your father, and maybe you should have one. So, the choice is yours. We can place you with a family, not in Idaho, but near Deever, so you can finish your education in familiar surroundings."

I was floored.

There it was, an offer to end my long, weird association with NECorp, to lead something remotely resembling a normal life. I was about to say yes, but Mr. Hammond wasn't finished yet.

"I'd also like you to consider staying. It really is only for a little while, and you'll be surprised how quickly it passes.

If you left, it would be our loss. You humanize us, Jaiden, in wonderfully unpredictable ways. If it hadn't been for you, we might still be run by Ted Bungrin."

That was heavy. I still wanted out, but I thought it would be rude to just jump on the offer, so I said, "Can I think about it?"

"Of course. I'm glad it's a question. It means you do think of us as a family in some ways. That's a feeling I want to promote in everyone here, make us feel we're in it together. I even have a few ideas on how to accomplish that. Care to hear one?"

"Umm . . . okay."

He smiled. "Another idea from Japan. Some of their corporations have their highest-paid employee, the CEO for instance, receive as a salary no more than one thousand times that of the lowest-paid employee. All the salaries rise, or fall, together. Every single worker reaps the benefits of the company's success and shares in its loss. Brilliant idea, really. It made the place more of a family."

"And you want NECorp to do that?" I asked, a little excited by the idea.

He grinned. "Oh, no, no, no. That would be ridiculously expensive. I think we should just tell everyone that. Unofficially, of course, so we wouldn't be liable."

I had no idea where to begin telling him what was wrong with that.

Mr. Hammond just stuck his finger back in the water and smiled.

That's how I left him, looking at the pumped water cascading over the carved NECorp logo, and giggling.

I wondered if Desmond Hammond III fell in a forest and no one was there to hear him, if he'd make a sound.

Still, I had to remind myself there was worse out there.

School was still a little weird, but at least I didn't have Tony following me around. He was busy doing the talk-show circuit, explaining how he'd saved us all from Bungrin and how he hoped to play himself in the film.

The excitement concerning my true identity had blown over. I still got some stares in the hall, but these days, it was more about people asking me to do things, like go to their birthday party, or star in the student production of a play called *How to Succeed in Business Without Really Trying*. I was interested, until I found out you had to sing.

Jenny and I were given an extra week for our bio project. Even though we met every day after school, we never seemed to manage to work on it, because now, we were what they call an item. They say first relationships don't last more than a few months, but I think you do some special bonding when you get shot at with someone, and I've got this feeling that no matter what, Jenny and I will always be close.

Speaking of bonding, that night, after I picked up Jenny,

we went to Nate's to meet for the movie, and I saw where he lived for the first time ever—a "normal" home. It was this nice big colonial, much messier but not so different from the corporate house I borrowed a billion years ago. And here's the thing: As he led us into his room, Jenny and I had to look at each other. There were all these corporate logos everywhere—on sneakers, T-shirts, pants, posters, half-full drinking glasses. Everywhere.

It made me realize that maybe I wasn't so different after all, that one way or another maybe everyone was being raised by corporations. Maybe someday kids will ask each other what company they're with more often than which country they're from. Corporations are just unavoidable. I mean, think about how big they are. A decade or so ago, when McDonald's and Burger King switched from styrofoam packaging to biodegradable paper, there was a measurable drop in the number of landfills worldwide. When they switched to a healthier oil? I bet there was a measurable increase in the average life expectancy of U.S. citizens.

Now, thank heaven for the Hulk and Gandhi, but *that's* power.

So I figured I might as well stay at NECorp.

Maybe because I was used to it, maybe because I didn't really want to break in a new family that would be looking at me cross-eyed anyway because of the money I'd have one day. I think Bungrin was right about one thing: anytime you bring something into the world, it gets dirty, so being normal couldn't really be as cool as I thought.

Maybe there is no normal.

Aside from that, stopping the mercury pollution, even though it was a drop in the bucket of a big bad world, made me feel like I'd actually done something important.

So I sort of made my peace with NECorp.

Which brings me to something Shakespeare wrote. He's been on my mind since we started reading him in Mr. Banyon's English class. There's this quote from one of his plays I really like. I didn't get it from the one we read, but while I was working on a paper I found this whole Web site of famous Shakespeare quotes. I think that's his best stuff, really, the quotes. His plots are kind of boring. Anyway, there was this one I really like:

> Full fathom five thy father lies;
> Of his bones are coral made;
> Those are pearls that were his eyes:
> Nothing of him that doth fade
> But doth suffer a sea-change

I like the idea that you just change and keep changing, even after you die, like there's no one finally judging you, or some lasting final end to the whole thing.

So, you don't ever really love Big Brother, you don't ever commit suicide.

You just change. And eventually, even Big Brother will change.

Speaking of change, when I do get that forty million? I'm going to ask for it in pennies. I doubt that's actually an option, but I'm going to ask just the same.

ACKNOWLEDGMENTS

The ever-witty Ambrose Bierce, in *The Devil's Dictionary*, once defined a corporation as an ingenious device for obtaining individual profit without individual responsibility. Not being a corporation myself, the responsibility here is mine, and while that's a fact that brings pride, I'd be remiss if I didn't mention those whose able assistance likewise made *Teen, Inc.* possible.

So, many thanks to my agent, Diane Bartoli of the Artists Literary Guild, for her terrific advocacy and wonderful professionalism, and to my editor, Mary Gruetzke, for acquiring the title, for her skillful edits and suggestions, for putting me in touch with fellow writer Corrine Demas upon my move to Amherst, and for generally being a delight to work with throughout the process.

My life as a writer has seldom been blessed with an evenly paced flow of assignments, and it so happened that many, many due dates coincided with that of *Teen, Inc.*, so an extra-special thanks to sister-in-law extraordinaire Sheila Kinney for reviewing the entire book in its rough form and more than adequately compensating for my sloppy typing.

Lastly, a familiar debt of gratitude to my pals at the Who Wants Cake crit group (Dan Braun, Nick Kaufmann, Sarah Langan, K. Z. Perry, and Lee Thomas), who reviewed the first few chapters of Jaiden's plight in nascent form and encouraged me to go on—with an extra shout-out to Nick for reading some later chapters that were bugging me. Hi, Nick!